His For Five Nights

Barrington Billionaires Series

Book Five

by
Jeannette Winters

Author Contact

website:
JeannetteWinters.com

email:
authorjeannettewinters@gmail.com

Facebook:
Author Jeannette Winters

Twitter:
JWintersAuthor

Newsletter Signup:
www.jeannettewinters.com/newsletter

Also follow me on:

BookBub:
bookbub.com/authors/jeannette-winters

Goodreads
goodreads.com/author/show/13514560.Jeannette_Winters

Alex Henderson needs to know the truth about his mother, even if it means exposing the family's darkest secret to the world.

Ziva Gryzb will do anything to stop the human trafficking ring that is terrorizing her country. She wasn't able to save her older sister, but she is determined to save other young women from the same fate.

Alex finds it will take more than money to gain answers. Willing to risk it all, including his reputation, he pretends to follow in his father's footsteps.

When Ziva hears yet another Henderson is on the prowl in her country, she sets out to take him down.

Alex doesn't expect an adversary to be his only hope. Ziva doesn't think she can defend, never mind love, a Henderson. Will the key to their hearts also be the key to their freedom or will they pay the price for a crime neither committed?

Copyright

Print Edition

An original work of Jeannette Winters, 2017.

All Rights Reserved. No part of this book may be used or reproduced in any manner whatsoever without written permission from the author, except in the case of brief quotations embodied in critical articles and reviews.

This book is a work of fiction. The names, characters, places, and incidents are products of the writer's imagination. Any resemblance to actual persons, places, events, business establishments or locales is entirely coincidental.

Dedication

This book is dedicated to my entire support team. You all have laughed and cried with me as this series continued. Know that I appreciate each and every one of you. You rock!

Karen Lawson, Janet Hitchcock, E.L. King and Marion Arche, my editors you are all amazing!

To my readers who continue to inspire me with endless messages and kind words. Always make time for romance.

Hate to say goodbye to your favorite characters? The perfect solution is a **Synchronized Series!** One world. Three authors. Character cross-over. Triple the amount of books. Binge reading at it's best.

Each author's books are full stories you can enjoy individually! But putting them all together weaves an even more pleasurable reading experience.

Chapter One

"You're a damn fool going there without any backup."

Alex Henderson didn't need or want Bennett Stone's approval. This trip was his decision to make. "I don't remember asking your opinion."

Bennett snorted. Running his hand through his hair he said, "You're a grown-ass man, and if you want to go out there and get yourself killed, I won't try to stop you. But I'm marrying your sister. If you do something this stupid, you won't be the only one to pay the price. Your brothers and Zoey will too."

"You're not stopping me," Alex said firmly.

"I'm not out to stop you. Just want to talk some sense into that thick Henderson skull of yours. Sit down with Brice. Maybe he'll move the timetable up."

Alex shot Bennett a look of doubt. Anyone who knew his oldest brother, Brice, would know he didn't budge once he set his mind to something. *Guess that's a common trait we share.*

"I don't want anyone to know what I'm doing." *Not*

sure how you found out. Alex didn't have to ask Bennett if he'd shared the knowledge. If he had, it would've been a family intervention instead of just the two of them.

"Lying to your brothers is something I mastered a few years back."

Alex knew his brothers weren't the only ones Bennett had lied to. He'd experienced that firsthand. Deceit wasn't something he tolerated, which was funny because most of his existence was a lie. *But that was business.* If Bennett's lack of truth had been for any reason other than to protect Zoey, the family would've cut him down in a heartbeat. *I still might if you cross me.* "Then we have an understanding."

Arching a brow, Bennett said, "Only if that means you agree not to go alone."

He was thirty-eight years old, and never had anyone watched his back before. No matter what Bennett might think, Alex wasn't about to let anyone, even someone highly trained in the art of protection, in on what he was really about to do.

Bennett was right, he was a damn fool for going in like this, but there was no other way. The answers were in Tabiq, and something held Brice back from making the trip himself. He could ask, yet the answer wasn't going to change anything. The rest of the family might not be interested in finding their mother, but Alex wasn't going to stop until he did.

"Bennett, you work for my brother. I don't need you there so you can report back to Brice."

"It's not about wanting me along. It's you needing me to cover your ass. You have no idea what you're walking into. These people hate the Hendersons."

Alex stared at him. "Tell me why you should come, and then I'll decide if you can accompany me." He knew it was a slim shot that Bennett would actually open up. If he didn't, he'd get the answers in Tabiq. It was only a matter of time. He could see how reluctant Bennett was to divulge what he knew. "Talk or get out."

Bennett finally opened his mouth. "You better sit down for this."

Alex looked at his watch. The jet was fueled and waiting. He didn't need a lengthy discussion, but if Bennett was going to say anything worthwhile, he wouldn't miss it. Walking back over to his desk, he pulled out the chair and took a seat.

"What do you know?" Bennett asked.

"You're talking. I'm listening," Alex growled.

"You already know where your mother was born. I'm still working on it, but so far, I haven't had any luck locating your mother or the others. People there are not very forthcoming. It's going to take time, but we'll get the answers one way or another."

Alex raised a brow. "Others?"

Bennett nodded. "This is why Brice is hesitant about going to Tabiq."

"Nothing will stop me from finding our mother."

"Mothers."

"I know how this works. One mother. One father."

"One father, six mothers."

Alex wasn't prepared for that news. It made sense to him as they all had a slight resemblance, but no two of them looked alike. "Are you positive?"

"Yes. I have the DNA proof. Each of your mothers was born and raised in Tabiq."

That didn't make any sense. Why would his father choose six different women? Was it just to avoid getting married? He could understand that because no woman would've been able to tolerate his ass. That didn't explain why they never came looking for their children. *For me.*

"I know we're miserable fucks, but you're telling me that out of six women, not one of them wanted us? Why?"

"It wasn't about wanting you or not. These women weren't given a choice."

So many things ran through his head. He didn't want to jump to conclusions because so many of them were ugly as hell. When it came to his father and business, nothing was off limits. Was he that sick and controlling in women's personal lives as well? *God knows he was when it came to us kids. Why not with girlfriends? Unless they weren't girlfriends. Money could buy a lot of things. Even silence.*

"Either tell me, or I'll find out when I get there." Alex had decided long ago that, no matter what the truth was, he wanted to know. He hoped that wasn't about to change. The look in Bennett's eyes said this was difficult for even him to say.

"Tabiq is corrupt. Young woman are seen as business deals."

"Are you saying they—?"

"Their young virgins are offered for a price. One your father was willing to pay. Six times."

Alex considered himself a strong man, but this was a sick, painful blow he wasn't expecting. He felt physically ill. *Dad, you . . . bought our mothers?* He'd come across a human trafficking ring before when doing research. It had disgusted him as it should any normal human being. Knowing he was conceived through such an act was abhorrent. *Why would a man so damn disgusting like my father even have one child, never mind six?* "Brice know?"

Bennett nodded.

Alex rose from his chair; it tipped backward and crashed to the floor. "And he's done nothing to stop it? What the fuck is he waiting for? We need to go and find them. Get them the hell out of there. Fucking kill whoever sold them to my . . . father."

The last word almost choked him to say. He never hated being the son of James Henderson more than he did at this moment.

"Alex, it's not that simple. Think about it. You're the third child, and you're thirty-eight. Your mother could be fifty-six now. It's been going on for over forty years. And it's an ongoing issue."

"Then we go there, and if they won't stop, we fucking crush them."

Bennett raised his hand. "No one is going to listen to

you. None of you. The people fear the Henderson name to this day. I never met your father, but he was one sick bastard. If he wasn't already dead—"

"You'd need to get in line."

Alex never thought he could hate his father more than he already did. Right now, hate wasn't strong enough to reflect his inner turmoil. He'd never felt out of control, but right now, he needed to stay away from the family. Seeing them, especially Brice, was going to open the floodgates to a conversation no one wanted to have.

He wasn't about to wait on Brice's approval to act. The wheels were already turning on what he needed to do. Bennett wasn't going to like it, but if they wanted answers, then they would have to use what they had in their favor.

"Bennett, if you're coming, we're doing this my way. Understood?"

"I don't like the look on your face, Alex. What the hell do you have planned?"

"You said they wouldn't welcome us because of who I am, and they're afraid of repercussions. Let's use that to our benefit and go for the jugular. Let them think I'm just like my father, and in the market for . . ." He couldn't say it.

"A virgin? You think you can pull that off when you can't even say the word?" Bennett asked, his voice filled with doubt.

"You'd be amazed at what I can pretend to be." Bennett didn't need to know how he'd come to be so talented. It had taken years of practice. First as a child hiding what he didn't want James to know and then as he became a successful published author of espionage novels. He'd managed to hide his true identity as an author from not only the readers but his own family.

"I guess you're coming," Alex said in a displeased tone.

"My team and I. When this goes dangerously critical, and it will, we're going to need backup."

"I'm trying *not* to bring attention to myself. The last thing I need is someone going in with guns blazing. My father never traveled with security guards, so I'm not about to either." *God knows my father should've. He was the most hated man I knew. Can't believe he lived long enough to die of natural causes.* "I want them to trust me. Not question my motives."

It was funny because no one had trusted James, especially not his children. Alex usually looked forward to the challenge of pretending to be someone he wasn't. This time, it scared the hell out of him. Was it because of how evil James was, or the fear that he might find he plays the role too fucking well? *I'd rather be dead than be anything like my father.*

"You're going to want those guns. Doug Atwood and I didn't receive a warm welcome when we went. Tabiq looks peaceful from afar, but I'm telling you, if they find out this is a hunting mission, we're dead, and your money won't buy a way out for us."

Alex arched a brow. Bennett didn't appear to be

bluffing. "You might want to stay behind. My sister won't forgive me if anything happens to you."

"If something happens to me, trust me, you won't be around to feel her wrath either. If we do this, we do it together. No man left behind."

Bennett never left the honor instilled in him as a Marine. Although Alex never walked in those boots, he'd heard the saying, Once a Marine always a Marine. After meeting Bennett, that saying became clear. Right now, it was the loyalty Alex needed, and a code he respected. "Let's do this."

Bennett didn't move. "This isn't about me or you *or* your mother. There are women, families, who will be affected if we fuck this up. It's more than just our lives on the line here. I will organize men to be on standby."

Alex had been so focused on his mother he'd missed the big picture. It was good to have Bennett around to bring that to light. That didn't mean he wanted more of the same, tough bastards hovering with guns. One was bad enough.

"I don't want anyone knowing what's going on. Or why my family is involved." Alex wasn't sure if he could stop it from leaking out to the rest of the world, never mind his family, but he'd try.

Bennett said, "The Turchetta family would be the perfect people for this and could get in and out in days. You don't need to be there. Let me make some calls."

There was no doubt that Bennett and the people he knew were able to pull off shit that most couldn't. His family had witnessed it a few times over the past two years. If he said the Turchettas were who they needed, it made sense to use them. But this wasn't about who was best for the job. This was personal. Something he needed to do himself. *I want my mother to know I found her, that I looked for her. Not someone on my payroll.*

"If that's the case, why hasn't it happened already? What are you waiting for?"

Bennett shot him a look, and he knew exactly the issue. Brice hadn't given his go-ahead. As far as Alex knew, Bennett hadn't shared what he'd learned with anyone other than Brice, but then again, Alex had been kept out of the loop. *Not sure if it was on purpose or not.* Alex knew if they were waiting on Brice, they could be waiting a long time. He never acted until he had every fact. That was the problem with being the scientific one. It had to have a logical order or it didn't happen. *Won't take action till he knows her name and location. It could be too late by then. It's not a cushy life in Tabiq. Who knows what kind of life my mother has had? If she's happy or sad, or hell, if she's healthy. I'm not going to wait until she's six feet underground before I make my move.*

He didn't knock his brother for the way he liked to handle things, but Brice had a hard time accepting that others functioned differently. *He's just going to have to deal with it, 'cause it's not all about him this time.*

Alex was a risk-taker. Every plan he'd ever tried to carve in stone went to hell. He was the fly-by-the-seat-of-your-pants type. No one would change that about him.

He liked his lifestyle and anyone who didn't could just shut the fuck up. He didn't want to hear other opinions, because he was set in his ways and didn't care what they thought.

"I want to go. This is *my* mother we're talking about. I don't need someone doing what I can do myself."

Bennett sighed heavily. "You're as stubborn as your brothers."

"Better believe it," Alex said firmly.

"It's not a compliment. It's going to get one of you killed one of these days."

"It's going to get me answers I need. That's all I care about right now," Alex growled.

"I must be just as fucking stupid, 'cause I'm going with you."

"No. Zoey is pregnant and needs you here." Alex wasn't just saying that because he wanted to do this alone. Zoey was expecting their first child. Although Alex wasn't a doctor, he could see she didn't look well. When he asked her about it, she said it was just morning sickness. The way Bennett hovered over her all the time said it was something more. There was no way he could risk Bennett being thousands of miles away if Zoey needed him. That didn't mean he was going to allow the Turchettas, or anyone else he didn't know, to get involved. *I was planning on doing this solo anyway. Why change that now?*

"I'll have Tessa, Lena, and Morgan watch out for her. We're not going to be gone that long. In and out, remember?"

He'd wanted to be gone already. It was becoming evident that Bennett wasn't going to let up. "Remember, no one can know where we're going." Alex shot Bennett a warning look.

"That's the way I roll. My bag's in the limo out front."

Cocky bastard.

Alex bent down, grabbed his suitcase, and headed for the door. His head remained filled with more shit than he could process. At first, he hadn't been looking forward to the long flight ahead of him. Now he knew he needed it. It was going to take all the self-control he could muster to pull this off. *Pretend to be like my father. A lowlife scum-sucking bastard.*

Ziva Gryzb hated holding back. Knowing a Henderson was back on Tabiq soil—and all she could do was sit back and wait—was killing her. Thankfully, it wasn't James, but it was still one of his evil sons, Alexander.

Her hands trembled as she gripped the steering wheel. He walked into the hotel holding his head high, as though he was welcomed here. She was sickened, thinking of how many bastards before him had come to this place for the same purpose. Their money paved the way, so almost everyone in power turned a blind eye to the dehumanizing behavior.

She needed to remind herself he was only here because her country was greedy and catered to his request.

That's why they come. Why he came. Because no one here will tell you no. Or so you think, Mr. Henderson. I'm here. I may not be able to stop everyone, but I will stop you. That I promise.

Her heart ached. Not for herself, but for her sister, Isa, who had fallen victim to such monstrous practices years ago. She barely remembered what Isa was like; she was so young when she disappeared. Nights of hearing her mother cry herself to sleep in sorrow still echoed through her soul. Her mother was never the same after that. *None of us were.*

She hated thinking back to those days, and hearing the name Henderson brought it all back as though it were yesterday.

It hadn't been all terrible. Her childhood had seemed normal. She had friends and played outside until the sun went down each day. As she grew older, things began to change. Not just for her either. All the neighbors seemed to have the same issue. The smiles that once lit their faces faded. She was lucky to see any of her friends outside, and even then, it was brief and they weren't allowed to speak.

Her father, Jaysin, also changed. He became overly protective and never let her out of his sight. One night she heard her parents whispering and her mother crying. Her father had said, "You know what will happen if we don't do this."

A few days later, on her sixteenth birthday, normally a special day for a young lady, her father took her for a ride far away from home. Everything about that night was still crystal clear. It was the day she said goodbye to not just her childhood but to life as she'd known it.

There were boxes and bags in the back of the truck. Her father hadn't spoken the entire trip. When they finally stopped the truck, they were at a cabin away from any sign of life. Her father explained he couldn't stay, and for her own protection, he needed to hide her. There were evil men who would come and take her from her family, and she'd be hurt. It had been the first time she'd been on her own. She'd been so innocent, naïve back then, and hadn't thought she'd survive.

But after weeks of tears and numbing fear, she found something inside her she hadn't known existed. Not only did she survive, she thrived in the solitude. She spent hours on end reading and educating herself more than she could've in their traditional education system. She read books most girls her age didn't have access to or would not have had time to read. It was as though she traveled the world and learned about different cultures right from her little sanctuary. When she wasn't reading, she kept herself physically fit. She'd make her way through the woods, down to the river, and swim against the current. Ziva knew she couldn't outmuscle a man, but she was going to be the best she could be if needed.

Her father had left her with a gun, which she had sworn she'd never touch. It'd sat there unloaded; she'd never been able to bring herself to think about holding it, never mind pointing it at another living being. What started out as scary, lonely, and terrifying, became a blessing. Each time her father came to check on her, he'd replenish her supplies and include new literature. If it hadn't been for the books, she'd have felt truly alone. Instead, she traveled the world through stories, learning about other lands and cultures. What she learned most was how to be a strong, independent woman.

Ziva grew tired of hiding. Over time, she figured out why her father hid her. Jaysin was afraid what had happened to Isa would also become her fate. After being hidden for almost two years, Ziva knew the time had come to break free from her hideaway. So on one of his trips to see her, she told her father her plan. She felt strong, and more importantly, she was determined.

Initially, her plan had appalled him. What father would willingly declare his daughter wasn't a virgin and had been sent away to give birth to a child? Her intelligent but grief-stricken father eventually conceded and saw wisdom in her plan, although it had taken several trips to convince him the lie could work.

When he finally agreed she returned home and fully realized how her father had saved her. He'd saved her from being taken in the night and sold like property to the highest bidder. *Sold to bastards like Henderson.*

She took a job as a secretary at the local police department so she was close and could overhear things she otherwise wouldn't be privy to. When she heard them say Alexander Henderson was here and wanted to talk business, she knew darn well what he wanted. *And there is no way in heck he is going to get it.*

Alex closed the door to the hotel behind him and seemed to be looking around. Had he noticed her following their taxi from the airport or when she parked several cars behind him? She'd tried keeping her distance, but she was no spy. Covert operations weren't her forte. That didn't mean she hadn't picked up a lot of techniques by working at the police station.

Ziva couldn't help but notice he didn't look like the pictures of his father. Adjusting the binoculars, she focused on his eyes. They were dark, but they weren't hard as she'd expected. *Especially with the reason for your trip here. I would think you'd be wearing sunglasses covering those eyes in shame. But then again, maybe you don't feel anything, just like your cold, immoral father.*

She questioned her sanity. All these years she'd been training and preparing to make a move and bring down one of these men. The police department didn't know the extent of her strength. Her knowledge. So, here she was, about to take on one of the richest and most powerful families by herself.

She knew there was no way Alexander could see her, but when his eyes looked her direction, a chill ran through her. It was ridiculous because it wasn't just Alexander she needed to worry about. The police were working hand in hand with the government to provide the ladies to the creeps. All it would take was the wrong person to see her spying on the hotel or Alexander, and she would disappear, no different than anyone else who questioned the treatment of their young women.

Lowering the binoculars, she closed her eyes for a minute. *This stunt is beyond crazy. How do I expect to pull this off?* Doubt was slowly taking over. If she allowed it to persist, she was sure to fail. Failure meant whatever young woman was about to be delivered to that bastard would have no chance of escape. *I'm her only hope. God help us both.*

She needed to get inside and make contact with him. Exactly how that was going to happen wasn't clear. Ziva ran a few scenarios through her mind. No matter what, it would look suspicious.

I have to pretend to be the virgin. The one he's expecting to be delivered. It sounded easy, but the women were normally eighteen years old. Here she was, twenty-nine and far from looking all young, sweet, and innocent. If there was any way she thought she could pull it off, she would go for it. Although she could pass for a few years younger, eighteen wasn't going to happen. *If he takes one look at me, he'll be demanding his money back.* He wasn't young, and it made her sick, thinking a man of his age would so callously take a young girl's life away.

She had to cross that plan off the list. The only thing she could do was watch and wait. Henderson held all the cards right now, and she felt helpless.

It was now or never. She opened the door to her truck and headed toward the hotel. Once inside, she noticed Alexander was still at the front desk, discussing something quietly with the hotel manager. *I don't want to know, so I hate that I have to know.*

She gingerly made her way closer, grabbed a magazine, and with her back to them both, pretended to be reading. It was a pathetic attempt as no one else was in the lobby. She stood out like a sore thumb, standing so close to them.

However, they were oblivious to her. *Not surprising. I'm not what he's into. Not young enough. Not innocent.*

In Tabiq, women her age were normally married with children. She often wondered what her life would've been like if her father hadn't hidden her away. Would she have found someone who'd love her, even though she wasn't a virgin? Had her father done things differently, she'd have suffered the same fate as many girls did. *Or like my Isa. Sold and never to see again. No one would know what happened to me.*

But her father had protected her, and because of his actions, she had a chance for a full life. Not the quiet family one, but a good one nonetheless. And she was determined to help other girls, other families, avoid the grief her family had.

Marriage was still out of the question. Her reputation was ruined by her own choice and lies. It had been a necessary evil. *I did what I had to do, and I'd do it all over again if it means I can stop this madness.*

Ziva didn't consider herself lonely. She thought of herself as driven. It might not be the dream most women around here had, but then again, it was better than the nightmare so many were living. *Choices. At least, I had one to make.*

"You want an adjoining room?" Ziva heard the manager ask.

"Yes."

"And the name of the occupant in the room?" he asked Alexander.

"My name on both," Alexander replied.

"Out of the ordinary, but whatever pleases you."

Ziva heard the manager's remark and knew exactly what he meant. How she wanted to turn around and tell him off. It would ensure instant gratification, but the price was too steep. She refused to threaten her one opportunity. Forcing herself to stay calm, she inched a step toward them.

The heel of her shoe caught on something, and she tumbled backward, landing flat on her back. When she looked up, Alexander had turned and was already bending over to assist her. Her natural instinct was to scream and tell him to keep his filthy hands off her.

Biting her lip, she pretended to be dazed.

"Miss, are you okay?" How could a monster's voice be soft and his concern genuine? *He's a liar, Ziva. Liars know how to mask their depravity.*

The only thing hurt was her pride, what little she had left. "I'm fine. Thank you."

She tried to get up, but he wasn't going to allow her to do so without his helping hand. Smiling, she placed her slender hand in his, and he easily pulled her to her feet. When she looked down, she noticed there was a raised stone on the flooring. Alexander must have noticed the same thing she did, because he barked at the manager.

"What the hell are you trying to do? This woman could've cracked her skull open on this stone floor. How are you going to compensate her?"

She stood there wide-eyed as the manager glared at her. There was no way he would open his wallet or anything else to her. He would easily identify her as Tabiqian. It wasn't as simple as what she wore, because they dressed in Western attire. It was the subtle downcast of her eyes from his first contemptible stare. No matter how she wanted to be bold and braver, she knew her place, and most of all, so did he. "You shouldn't be here, woman. You tripped because you are clumsy," he hissed in their native tongue even though in Tabiq they also spoke fluent English.

There was so much she wanted to say to him, but her mouth remained shut. Even though she could've responded in her native language, it would've been out of character and brought more unwanted attention onto her.

Turning from her, the manager said, "Is this woman with you, Mr. Henderson? Because we don't allow loitering here." The manager looked her up and down, shook his head, and said sternly, "Be gone and do not come back here. Do you hear me?"

Ziva had no choice but to comply. If the manager called the police, not only would she be physically removed, she'd be fired as well. She nodded, but to her surprise Alexander interrupted.

"The second room is for this young lady." Alexander's next words sounded more like a threat. "I'm sure no one will be questioning her again."

The manager averted his eyes from meeting Alexander's and nodded. "I'm so sorry, sir. It will not happen again."

"I believe the apology belongs to her, not me."

The manager, still with his head lowered, said in English, "I beg your pardon, miss."

He may have acted as though he was sorry, but when he looked up, Ziva didn't miss the hatred lying deep within him. Alexander might hold power over things now, but she didn't want or need his protection. The last thing she could afford was to be in debt to him. He was and always would be nothing more than her enemy.

Alexander reached out, took hold of her elbow, and guided her past the manager. Once out of earshot he asked, "What's your name?"

She was tongue-tied.

"You have one, I'm sure," he said sarcastically.

Oh, she knew *her* name; it was whether or not she wanted him to have the real one. Lying was easy, but if they encountered anyone who knew her she'd blow her cover. "Ziva Gryzb. And yours?" *Not that I need it.*

He smiled and said, "Alex. I don't know what you're doing here, but the room is yours. Feel free to use it." He reached out his hand and dropped a room key into hers.

"Mr.—"

"Alex."

She nodded. "Alex. Thank you for what you did, but I cannot take a room from you. It would look . . ." *Like I'm the one you are having sex with.*

"You should've thought about that before you decided to eavesdrop on my conversation with the manager."

She blushed. "I'm sorry. That was very disrespectful of me." Although she didn't have any respect for the man, she had some for herself.

"May I ask why you were listening?" Alex asked, his brow arched.

Think fast. Come on, Ziva. You've been waiting for this day, and you can't blow it in the first few minutes. "News travels fast around here of a newcomer, and I wanted to meet you. Guess I could've chosen a more subtle way." She forced a light laugh.

He chuckled as well. "Well, Ziva Gryzb, you do know how to make a memorable first impression. I guarantee you're not someone I'll soon forget."

His eyes roamed over her as he spoke. She wanted to be angry, but for some unexplainable reason, her body reacted to his look. That infuriated her. Now red-faced and confused she said, "I can't say the same about you."

With that, Ziva turned and left the hotel. When she got back in the truck, she realized the hotel room key was still in her hand. Smiling that something actually went right with this day she slipped the key into her pocket. *I may need this to keep an eye on your disgusting ass.*

Chapter Two

Although he found her to be a sweet distraction, he wished Ziva hadn't interrupted his conversation with the manager yesterday. The hotel manager wasn't the man in charge, but he was the only contact he had. Alex had hoped to encourage the manager to let him speak to his boss right away; he wasn't one who liked waiting around. Since that conversation hadn't taken place, he was now stuck in a hotel room, waiting for the manager to "deliver the goods."

Recalling how coldly the man had spoken about the women he could choose from infuriated Alex, but it was more than that. He would like to take a match and burn the hotel to the ground. This hellhole was the same place his father had come all those years ago. His own mother had been one of the women mistreated, sold as a possession instead of a person. How many contemptible men had ignored the evil that occurred here?

He'd wanted to know why his father had been the man he was. Never in his wildest dreams had he imagined such sick and evil behavior. More than thirty years later, the Henderson name still caused people to tremble. Had his father returned here throughout the years, used more young girls, then simply tossed them aside? *I thought growing up under his thumb was bad enough. I guess we had the best of him, which doesn't say much. I can't think anything good about him at all.*

Alex couldn't help but think how his sister, Zoey, would feel if she knew what their father had done. He wasn't sure Bennett would share that type of knowledge with her. Alex knew Bennett loved his sister, and telling her the truth would cause more pain than she could handle in her condition.

Zoey must've suspected something; their father treated her differently from the boys. Although he hated them all, which he had no qualms reminding them, James had honed a deep resentment for Zoey. It was one Alex didn't understand until now. Having to raise a female, when he viewed them as worthless property, must've pissed him off. What Alex still needed to know was why he'd have children at all. *He didn't love us, and we sure as hell weren't conceived in love, so why the fuck do it? Why keep us? Were there more he hadn't kept?*

These weren't answers he could find here. With James dead, they'd probably never know. That didn't mean he'd stop searching, and that was something he'd need to do himself, not with Bennett.

Alex and Bennett traveled the last leg of the trip separately with Bennett flying on a commercial flight. Weapons wouldn't have made it through the airport.

That meant he and Bennett had to touch base so his backup would be armed and ready. Without anyone seeing them was going to be very difficult. This town was a close-knit community, and not much happened without being observed by someone. So much so they had to stay at different hotels. Alex laughed softly. *Not sure Bennett considers his lodging a hotel or a barn.*

He didn't feel too bad. Alex hadn't asked him to come, so whatever accommodation Bennett suffered through wasn't his concern. Making the people here believe he was like his father was his first priority.

Alex couldn't help but think back to the look on Ziva's face. She pretended she hadn't known his name, but he saw it in her eyes. *Pure disdain.* He understood why. James had given these people reason to hate him. Bennett spent hours updating Alex on everything he'd learned to date. Alex thought it couldn't get worse, but it did.

At one point, Alex had contemplated having the pilot turn the jet around, and flying back to Boston. Not because he was a coward. If anything, each new fact fueled his drive to move forward. He felt worse for one brother more than the others. Logan's mom had died birthing him. Bennett had reminded him of the big picture. It wasn't just one woman or one mother. The purpose of the expedition was to stop the evil still taking place in Tabiq. It was bad enough thinking it was only his father abusing the women of Tabiq, but this was much worse than he imagined. Knowing it was still happening today, outraged him. Even if he stopped it all, the families affected deserved some reparation.

Although it made him sick, he needed to keep that in mind. Anyone who approached him could potentially be involved in the human trafficking ring. The policy of innocent until proven guilty wasn't going to fly. From what they knew, the level of corruption was so deep it wouldn't break easily.

This area wasn't the first place he'd been that was evil and corrupt, but it sure as hell was the worst. Typically, he took time to seek decent people and befriend them. There was no time for that now. He needed to keep his distance from the locals, getting deeper involved than he already was would only hinder his efforts.

His mind wandered back to the intriguing woman he met yesterday. Ziva might have thought she was stealthy, but he'd picked up on her tail in that ratty old pickup truck at the airport. She had surprised him when she'd decided to follow him inside the hotel and had practically thrown herself at him. He wasn't foolish enough to trust her, but he didn't take her as a real threat either. *I hope that's not a mistake.*

It wouldn't be the first tale of a man being taken down by a stunning woman. *And that she was.* He'd lain awake last night, haunted by thoughts of her. He couldn't explain it, but he'd been instantly drawn to her. There was nothing about her he'd ordinarily find attractive. His preferred taste had always been blonde hair, and her hair was so dark it was almost black, reminding him of starling wings. The women he dated were tall with large breasts, not always real, but large nonetheless. Ziva was at least eight inches shorter than he was, and her small breasts matched her petite frame. Yet she had stood in front of him with such confidence he found it sexy as hell.

Logically he knew he should've let the manager throw her out on her ass. Instead, he handed over the key that was supposed to be for whoever they were going to bring him. Now he had no place for the other woman except in his room. *It'll look more the part, but damn, I don't like this. Not one bit.*

The air conditioner made a constant hum, drowning the outside noise. It also was impossible for him to hear if Ziva had taken him up on his offer and utilized the room. The taxi driver had informed him this was one of the best places in town because it had air conditioning. With the sweltering heat, he couldn't imagine she'd refused. Even if she didn't like him, a few days of relief from this one-hundred-five-degree temperature would appeal to anyone. *And it gives her the opportunity to keep a close eye on me.*

Alex pictured what Bennett would say if he knew what he'd done. When they parted ways, Bennett made it clear that under no circumstances should he deviate from the plan. Alex hadn't finished checking in, and their plan had already gone to hell. *Guess that's because I don't answer to Bennett. Haven't answered to anyone in a very long time.*

He heard the SAT phone that Bennett gave him ring, no need to check the caller ID.

"What's up?"

"Have they delivered her yet?"

Alex would like to correct Bennett, but his terminology was right. The girl wasn't coming on her own accord. "No."

"When do you expect her?"

"I was interrupted when speaking to the manager."

"What does that mean?" Bennett asked.

"Simple. We didn't finish the conversation." Alex saw no reason to go into details.

"Unless you enjoy baking in this god-awful heat, I suggest you handle that now," Bennett said, sounding aggravated.

"Heat's not bothering me one bit," Alex said, leaning back on the couch and smiling. He knew it was wrong, but he took pleasure knowing Bennett's accommodation didn't have AC.

"Good, then you wouldn't mind meeting me. You have what I need."

Alex knew exactly what that meant. He was looking for the duffel bag with an assortment of guns and ammunition in the closet. They anticipated Alex's room would be searched; it was best to get the bag out of there quickly.

"How do you plan on pulling this off? I'm unable to move without eyes on me."

There was a pause then Bennett answered, "I met a

taxi driver the last time I was here. Once he helped us, we had to get him and his family out of the country. Finding someone willing to risk it all is nearly impossible."

Ziva. Alex was shocked she was his first thought. For all he knew she'd rat them out for the right price. If that happened, Bennett was right: neither of them would make it back to Boston. *At least, not alive.*

"How good are you at picking locks?"

Bennett snorted. "I'm not a burglar."

"So that's a no?"

"I didn't say that. What do you need?"

"Wait until dark. I'll let you know when I go out. Whoever is watching me most likely will follow. I'll give you thirty minutes to get in and out."

"Roger."

Normally, he would've thought the guy was just a cocky bastard, but Alex had heard plenty about Bennett's skills. There wasn't much he couldn't do. Since arriving in Tabiq, he'd corrected his stance. Bennett had been right. This wasn't a place to come alone. At least, not if you're one of the good guys.

ZIVA COULDN'T BELIEVE the only thing separating her and Alex was an adjoining door. She purposely stayed quiet, so he didn't know she was there. It was hard because the man didn't seem to sleep. She'd pressed her ear against the door at all different hours, and each time he seemed to be pacing.

He may not need sleep, but I do. Her eyes were burning from exhaustion, yet she knew if she closed them, that would be the time he left his room. She needed to get inside his room and search for proof of why he was there. *Not that I need it. He's a Henderson. We all know why he's here.*

She was just about to lie down on the bed when she heard something like a door closing in the hallway. Ziva dashed to the door and wished there was a peephole so she could see. Pressing her ear to the door, she heard footsteps, but they stopped right outside her door. She held her breath, not that he could hear, and waited. Was he going to knock? Did he have a key and was about to come in?

If he does, what's the problem? He gave me the key. He offered me the room. That didn't mean she wanted to see him, especially not in her room. She'd kept her emotions under wrap in the lobby yesterday, but in here, alone, would be much harder.

After what seemed to be an eternity, whoever it was must have changed their mind and walked away. When the footsteps seemed far enough away, she cracked her door slightly and peered out. She could tell it was Alex. His tall, muscular build wasn't something she could forget. *Even if I wanted to.*

Ziva watched him turn the corner and disappear from sight. This was her opportunity. She closed her door, ran to the dresser where she had placed the hard plastic bank card, then headed out the door.

She didn't have time to waste. He was gone but for how long she wasn't sure. *Hopefully not to go and meet up with some unsuspecting woman.* Ziva froze as her hand was on the doorknob of his room. Should she follow him instead? Would her planned search turn up empty and her time be better spent watching him?

Taking a deep breath, she took the card and slipped it between the doorjamb. Sliding it upward, it came in contact with the locking mechanism. It took a few tries, but eventually she heard the click, and the door opened.

That was her answer. She'd search now and follow later. Ziva quickly went into his room and shut the door behind her. She began opening drawers and looking through them. It was odd because he had hardly unpacked, as though he wanted to be ready to leave at a moment's notice. *Do your dirty little deed, have your fun, and leave. Oh yes, you're the son of James Henderson. God help the poor woman they send you.*

Ziva needed to focus on the task at hand. There wouldn't be a second shot at it. Looking around, she noticed she'd left the drawers ajar. She hadn't thought about keeping things exactly as she'd found them when she came in. All she wanted was proof of who he was, and what he was doing. She then could post her findings on the Internet for all the world to see exactly what kind of sick bastard he was.

She had every intention to make sure the Henderson name would never be looked upon in the same light in the business world. No respectable person would want any dealings with them. Their family name would go down in shame where it belonged.

Ziva thought about going back and fixing the contents of the drawers. That would waste valuable time. So instead, she made sure the next few things she searched were scattered around making it look as though his room had been ransacked. There was a small amount of money left on the nightstand, which she took to make it look like a robbery. *In this town, that's very likely. Even in the one decent hotel. But I'd be shocked if anyone besides me was stupid enough to mess with a Henderson.*

If the situation weren't so darn serious, she'd laugh. If her father had a clue what she was up to, he'd roll over in his grave. Although he'd always spoken about doing something to make the madness end, he never had the chance. Despite his many stories of what he'd wanted to do, she wasn't putting them into action. She would do things her way. For her sister. For her father. She wasn't delusional enough to believe it all would be over, but she was going to bring to light what was happening, what'd been going on for more years than she'd been alive. No one would look at Tabiq and their women the same again. *Money won't buy my silence.*

Ziva headed to the closet. When she opened it, she found blankets from the bed piled up in a ball. She pulled them out and noticed they'd been intentionally placed to hide a duffel bag that didn't match the rest of his luggage. That was odd. The bag seemed completely out of place. She bent down and tried to drag it out, but it was too heavy. She knelt down and unhooked the first belt around it. Alex certainly wanted whatever was inside to be secure.

She knew this had to be what she was looking for. Once it was unlatched, she moved the zipper down and reached her hand inside. Ziva gasped, as her fingers made contact with cold metal. Running her hand carefully down, she knew it was a gun. Moving her hands around, she noticed there wasn't just one.

What the heck is he doing with all this? Is he going to kill the women after he gets what he wants from them? It was truly a horrible life for these women after being forced to have sex with these disgusting men. Some probably thought death was easier than living a life in disgrace afterward. No man would marry them. They were forced to continue a life of prostitution or live alone in abject poverty. They couldn't go back to their families; they didn't want to bring shame to them either. *Maybe death is a merciful thing, but I refuse to allow Alexander Henderson to deliver it.*

Ziva wasn't sure how she was going to manage, but the bag was going with her. She stood, grabbed the handles, and with all her might began to pull it from the closet floor. *You must have an arsenal in here. It's got to weigh over one hundred pounds.*

Her hands hurt as she struggled to move it a few inches at a time. This wasn't going to work. Since she was all about keeping her own room secure, she'd never unlocked the adjoining door on her side and she couldn't drag a large heavy bag back to her room through the hallway. It was too risky. With all her effort it still lay partially in the closet. She closed it and put the blankets back on top. She needed to find someone to help her, someone she could trust.

There were good people here, and she knew it. They hated what was going on as much as she did. The only difference: they had families who'd pay the price if they helped her. She had no one left. After spending two years in hiding, Ziva hoped to spend many years making up for lost time with her parents. Instead they'd died not long after she came out of hiding, tearing her heart in two. There had been no explanation about what happened, but she knew they'd been searching for answers about her sister, Isa. *Not surprising.* She'd buried them alone, lived alone, mourned alone. Years later, nothing had changed. No one would cry for her if she disappeared. *No one would mourn.*

Closing the closet, she headed toward the door and heard the handle jiggle. *Oh, God. He's back.* She looked around the room for a place to hide. If she'd thought about it earlier, she'd have unlocked her side of the adjoining door. It would've been the easiest way of escape. Since she had decided to keep it bolted on her side, using it was impossible. There was a couch, but that wouldn't provide any cover. *What the hell am I going to do?*

Rushing over, she threw herself onto the floor and rolled beneath the bed. This was one time being so petite worked in her favor.

She lay there motionless as she heard the door open.

"Shit," a man's voice hissed.

Ziva could see the closet from her hiding spot. Although the room was a jumble, the guy seemed to head straight for the closet. That struck her as odd, but it meant he knew what he was looking for.

Although she couldn't see him, she saw his feet as he stopped and opened it. The blankets were tossed back onto the floor near the bed, blocking her view. Moments later, she heard the bag unzip.

Then it sounded like the bag was picked up, and the man was walking away. Whoever it was didn't seem worried about the room looking ransacked or if he should look for an intruder. She heard the room door open and close again, and she was alone. *He'd known exactly where to look and what to find. Was he working with Alexander Henderson or against him?*

Fearing someone could still be in the room, Ziva didn't come out of her hiding place immediately. After a few minutes, with no further sounds or movement, she pushed the blankets away and rolled out. Looking around the room, it appeared exactly the way she'd left it: a hot mess. He'd touched nothing except one thing. *One deadly bag.*

Her heart sank. There was nothing she could do to stop him, any more than she could Alexander. If she'd made a peep, one of those guns most likely would've been used on her. In this hotel the manager would turn a blind eye to her death, no different than he did to everything else going on here.

Saying goodbye to the guns wasn't an option either. She might not know where they were going, but she knew with that kind of firepower it wasn't for anything good.

With a heavy sigh, her entire body weakened with defeat. She had more questions than she'd had before. *Is that guy working with or for Alex? Because if he is, I'm sure this is not the last I'll see of him. But if he's working for the government and collecting what they were promised in trade, the guns are long gone and so is he.*

Ziva couldn't picture they'd pass up money for arms, but in conjunction with bribing them, they most definitely would. She realized her first thought about Alex's plans for the guns was wrong. The sweetness she'd seen in his eyes was a façade. Alexander was worse than James. Not only was he here to feed his sick pleasure, but to deal in illegal weapons as well. *Tabiq didn't need any help getting more corrupt than it already was.*

Ziva wished she'd opened the bag to see what else was in it besides guns. From the weight, it could have been anything. The stakes had grown higher, and she was in way over her head.

Standing in his room wasn't going to accomplish anything. And if Alexander returned and caught her, she wouldn't leave anytime soon, if at all. She had a feeling he already questioned why she was around yesterday. He seemed oddly aware, as if he's known she was there.

Finding her here now would confirm his suspicions. Opening the door, she peered down the hallway. All was quiet, thankfully. Quickly she slipped out of his room, closed the door gently, and went back to her own room.

As she turned the lock on her door, she noticed her hands were trembling. Bringing her hand to her chest and covering it with the other, she tried to calm her nerves. Ziva was playing a dangerous game, and with people way out of her league. She'd thought she could use technology to bring these detestable activities to light. This ordeal wasn't as simple as snapping pictures and putting them on the Internet. This was about fighting to save innocent lives. *Maybe my own. He didn't give me this room freely. Do I stay to find out? This crazy plan may be the only way I find the proof I need. I just need to live long enough to share it with the rest of the world and pray someone out there cares enough to help.* A stream of tears rolled down her face as she walked to her bed.

Ziva, who only moments earlier had been exhausted and fighting to keep her eyes open, now lay on her bed forcing herself to memorize everything she could about Alex and the events that had taken place. She might be only one person, but she'd heard it enough in her life: it only took one to make a difference. If it were the last thing she did, she'd make him pay for what he was about to do. *And if I can, I'll stop you before you do it.*

Chapter Three

Alex didn't bother informing the manager what he'd returned to. Back in Boston, he would've had the place fingerprinted. Here, he didn't think it would matter if they had a name or picture of the person responsible. It was every man for himself in Tabiq.

He still couldn't believe the person was able to get in and out that quickly. Bennett must've been five minutes behind him and swore he passed no one. Alex wracked his brain, trying to recall seeing anyone in the lobby or the hall. Nothing came to mind. That could only mean one thing. The culprit had a room on the same floor as he did.

Alex needed to know who Ziva was. Why had she followed him? Given she was a local, why would she take him up on his offer to stay in the hotel? Surely she had a home somewhere. *Why follow me?* That room would be perfect for monitoring his coming and goings. But why would she care? Against Bennett's instructions, Alex went to her room and knocked on the door.

No one answered. He knocked again, harder this

time and called out, "Ziva, it's Alex." He heard the turn of the lock. When she opened it, he noticed the chain remained on the door so it only opened a few inches.

"Good morning."

Not really. "Good morning." He had intended to ask her if she'd seen or heard anything out of the ordinary last night. But, was Ziva hiding something? For all Alex knew, it could easily be a boyfriend. Whatever it was, he needed to know. "Do you think I can come in? I have something I'd like to discuss with you."

He could see the concern in her eyes. What did she think he was going to do to her? Surely she'd seen his concern for her yesterday, and how he'd—

Oh.

Of course.

I'm a Henderson.

I wouldn't open the door to me either. That wasn't going to stop him from pushing it further.

"Ziva, I have a key. I could've entered anytime if I wanted to harm you." Concern quickly became panic in her eyes. Alex knew his choice of words were stupid at best.

"Is that some kind of threat?" Ziva asked firmly, but Alex could hear her voice crack slightly.

He didn't enjoy manipulating her, but he had to do whatever necessary to get inside her room. If she wouldn't do it willingly, he'd kick the damn door down. She was hiding something. Either she was working with the guy who broke in yesterday, or she'd seen who it was.

Either way, Alex wanted answers.

He shouldn't be standing there, wasting time on this. If they'd have gotten the weapons, it would be something to take seriously, but this was more about his ego, and he knew it. Someone ransacking his room was chump change compared to the big fish they were going after.

Knowing that didn't change how he felt. When his eyes met hers, he could see she was hiding something or someone. That irked him. At that moment, he didn't care about anything other than getting into her room.

Finally, Ziva closed the door, and he heard the chain unlatch. When the door opened again, she allowed him in. With her hand on the knob, she gestured for him to enter, but the look on her face said she was doing so reluctantly. *Because I'm a man or because I'm a Henderson?*

Once inside, he scanned the room. It didn't look like she'd been there, never mind having anyone with her. The bed was pristinely made, and nothing at all showed occupancy.

"Are you alone?"

Her eyebrows rose. "Does it look like anyone else is here?"

Alex looked around again, knowing damn well there wasn't anyone else. "I had an issue with my room. Did you hear or see anyone?"

Although he didn't make it obvious, he was studying her body language as she replied. She instantly crossed her arms and averted her eyes. "I didn't hear anything last night. I'm a deep sleeper."

I don't remember saying it was during the night. So what did you hear? He walked to stand directly in front of her. She practically dropped her chin to her chest. Reaching out, he placed one finger under her chin and tipped her head so she faced him. "Nothing at all?" Alex asked softly.

Ziva closed her eyes before saying, "Your door may have opened a few times. But I didn't see anything. I was in . . . asleep early."

And the story changes. Heard nothing, now saw nothing. I wish it weren't true, but you, my dear Ziva, are a liar. A bad liar. Who are you lying for?

Dropping his hand, he said, "That's a shame. Something very valuable to me was taken out of that room. When I find the person responsible, they will wish they were dead."

Her eyes widened, and he watched as she swallowed hard. "I . . . I hope you recover your belongings."

Alex expected her to say he should've stored them away in the hotel safe with the manager instead of leaving them unprotected in his room. Or even where he was when whatever was taken. Yet, Ziva didn't ask any questions. *That's because you already know the answer.*

She gave herself away when she said the door opened several times and not just once. That meant she might've seen Bennett leave with the duffel bag. He hadn't planned on telling Bennett about Ziva, but with this new development, he had no choice. She became number one on his watch list. *And not because I find you sexy as hell either.*

His father had taught him young to keep his enemies close. Until he knew specifically what her game was, Alex wasn't going to give her any room to avoid him. "I haven't had breakfast yet. Join me." He didn't leave any room for a refusal, as he went to the door and held it open for her.

Ziva opened her mouth as though she wanted to tell him no, or better yet where to go, but said nothing, reached for her room key on the table, and walked out the door. *Wise choice. Your only one.*

As they made their way down the hall, Alex pulled out his SAT phone and texted Bennett. *Room 204.*

Roger.

Alex hated to do it, but they needed to know who she really was, and how big a threat she posed. She might be only five foot two, but if she was armed, she could be as lethal as anyone else they were about to mess with.

"If you have work to do, I'm okay with skipping breakfast."

Oh, I bet you are. Alex slipped the phone back into his pocket and said, "No. I cleared my schedule. I'm all yours for the day." He saw Ziva stiffen as she put on the prettiest fake smile he'd ever seen. *Not buying what you're selling.*

"My lucky day."

As they were about to leave the hotel, the manager called out, "Mr. Henderson. Your . . . package is scheduled to arrive around noon."

Shit. "Change of plans. Have it delivered tomorrow. Same time." Alex didn't wait for a response as he placed a hand on Ziva's elbow and ushered her out of the lobby.

"It sounded like your *package* was important."

He knew she was prying, and he wasn't divulging. "It can wait." Once outside, he hailed a taxi.

"Where to?" the driver asked as he opened the door for them.

Alex turned to Ziva and said, "This is your hometown. Take me somewhere a tourist wouldn't usually go."

Ziva muttered something in her language to the driver. He nodded and shut the door. Once inside, the driver pulled away from the curb, his tires squealing. It became evident quickly they were heading out of town. He was tempted to ask exactly where it was she was taking him, but he hoped it would be a pleasant surprise.

As civilization disappeared, he wished he'd kept one of those guns for himself. *Or at least had Bennett tail us. Two for two on bad plans so far. I'm on a streak of bad luck. It better end soon. If I make it back to the hotel in one piece today, I'm going to have to pull my head out of my ass.* He turned to Ziva, who sat quietly looking out the passenger's window. He could see a serious look on her face. Was she contemplating how she was going to dispose of his body after they killed him? There were reasons travel advisories appeared for Tabiq. They were known for being ruthless, cold people. Two things he couldn't picture Ziva as. *But if I were going to set a trap, I'd use someone as stunning as Ziva.*

Alex lived his life on the edge. His family would never believe it. He was a highly successful author. He took the time to do hands-on research, which was the reason he was so damn good at it. Each time his family thought he was away on some fancy vacation, he actually was deep undercover with some drug lord, arms dealer, or terrorist ring. There had been a few close calls when his cover was blown, and he'd been doubtful about making it out alive. He didn't want to just talk the talk. He wanted to walk the walk as well. *It'd be like a virgin writing a how-to-please-your-man manual. Interesting, but no proven facts.*

As they continued to drive farther away, all he could think was there are worse ways to die than at the hands of a beautiful woman.

ZIVA MIGHT BE able to control what was happening on the outside, but inside, she was shaking to the core. At least, in the adjoining rooms they were separated by a lock on each side of the door. Here in the taxi, there was nothing. If he pulled out a gun and forced her to do whatever, she'd be defenseless. *That doesn't mean I won't fight you with all my might.*

Her mind told her to be extremely cautious, the last thing she should do was be alone with him. Yet, here she was with him and a taxi driver, and by the looks of the driver, he'd side with Alex if anything went wrong. By the look on his face, when she told him where to drive them, he must have thought she was certifiable.

Crazy or not, Ziva had to do this. No matter how scared she was, or what he tried to make her believe, she still hoped she could talk Alex out of going through with what he had planned, but that was totally irrational. He was a Henderson. Men like him weren't swayed once they made up their minds. There had been something when they'd first met that held promise for him. *Something tells me you're not all bad. I'm just not sure if there's enough good in you to be saved. But I have to try.*

As far as she knew, this was his first trip to Tabiq. Even contemplating doing what he was about to do was morally wrong. Yet, Alex was expecting the virgin today, but he canceled so he could spend the day with her. She was positive it wasn't her charm or looks that garnered his attention. He was fishing for information. Ziva had none to give. He knew she'd noticed the mess in his room. That didn't mean she was going to admit to anything. If she could get him to stop today, maybe she could tomorrow too.

How she would pull that off wasn't clear. If she had to, she'd tie Alex up and make him listen to her rant about how wrong and sick it was to take advantage of helpless young women until it made it through his thick skull. Physically she was no match for him, and he knew it. *In his eyes, I'm no threat. How mistaken can he be?* She was driven by something more powerful than physical strength. He couldn't touch her when it came to motivation. Her anger, pain, and determination had been building for years. If she couldn't persuade Alex to stop and leave before he acted on his sick desire, then she'd make sure he paid the price. *And he has no idea what I'm capable of. Heck, I'm not sure I know.*

Ziva had many different emotions running through her. She wanted to make him pay, punish him, but something deep inside her wanted to save him. The conflict was tearing her apart inside. When she heard a Henderson was returning to Tabiq, she knew what needed to be done. She planned and was focused.

After meeting him, things weren't as black and white. Although the signs were there, she had to remind herself that he wasn't his father. She couldn't let what James Henderson did blind her to who Alex was. If she was going to play judge and jury, she needed the facts first. All she had now were her suspicions. She needed concrete evidence before making a decision. *Is he savable? Is he worth saving? Does he want to be saved?*

Her country didn't care about such things. The government didn't value its citizens. Justice was only a word in the dictionary. It held no meaning when it came to crimes. She hated the laws of her land. The abuse against women was ignored, or worse, condoned. Yet if someone was caught with a gun, it was punishable by imprisonment. Alex didn't need to know that. She wanted him to fear what his fate could be if he continued down this disgusting, immoral path.

Ziva wasn't sure if it'd change anything, but he needed to be warned that the prisons in Tabiq weren't like the ones in the United States. There was no Internet. No television. No air conditioning or visitation. And absolutely no privacy at all. *And no one to care if a brawl breaks out and you're killed. Just one less body for them to take care of.*

The facility was just beyond the horizon. It would appear in their view in a few minutes. It wouldn't take long for Alex to see the tall guard towers at the gate and also scattered throughout the prison. It was surrounded by a ten-foot fence with barbed wire circling the top.

As a secretary for the police department, she'd made this journey several times to deliver paperwork when a prisoner was approved for release. It was rare, but it happened. In most cases, once you saw the inside of this place, you would plan on dying there.

She'd heard rumors of people trying to escape. If the guards didn't shoot you, or the attack dogs catch you, the electrified fence took care of it. The people of Tabiq never had to worry about a hardcore criminal escaping, but with a corrupt government, she knew there were innocent people sentenced to life there, through no accident. Their only crime was not complying, or speaking out against the inhumanity of Tabiq. Ziva knew if *she* was caught doing this, she wouldn't have to worry about seeing the inside of the prison. This place was for men only. Women were handled in an entirely different way. *They deal with us swiftly and permanently. Our life sentence is short.*

This knowledge should be enough for her to stop the taxi, turn around, and pretend to have never met Alexander Henderson. Yet, she couldn't do it. She wanted, no needed, to break the cycle of immoral behavior. If she could make Alex see how wrong it was, maybe he would enlighten others. If the billionaires of the world didn't take part in such acts, her government wouldn't have a choice but to find an alternative income. *Hopefully a legal one.*

She waited for Alex to speak when the towers came in sight. It didn't take long.

"Not very romantic, are you?" Alex said, his tone dry as he stared straight ahead at the prison.

If circumstances were any different, she'd have laughed, but too much was at stake for even a grin. Although Alex's words didn't appear to be serious, the look on his face was.

"You wanted to see someplace that a tourist doesn't normally see. Unfortunately, some have. Once inside they're no longer considered a tourist but become a permanent resident of Tabiq, whether they like it or not. And trust me, Alex, they don't like it."

In her language, Ziva instructed the driver to pull onto the shoulder of the road and to get out of the vehicle. He did as she asked. She needed time to speak to Alex alone. If the driver overheard, he might turn her in. All would be lost at that point.

"I'm familiar with how prisons work."

"Even here in Tabiq? It's not a hotel, believe me."

Alex turned to face her. His dark eyes seemed to bore into hers as he stared. "Why did you bring me here, Ziva?"

This was her chance to tell him exactly why. She should be honest and lay it all on the line. Tell him she knew why he was here and what she thought about it. As she opened her mouth, panic filled her. *What if I tell him and he doesn't care? What if I'm wrong about him and there is nothing good inside? He could go back to the manager and tell him what I did, where I took him. I'd have signed my own death sentence.*

Ziva held her head high and said as confidently as she could, "I thought someone of your . . . intelligence might want to see all sides of Tabiq." *Since you seem to be interested in the ugly side, thought I'd show you a different view. One you might have to get used to.*

Sad thing was she knew he'd never see the inside of that prison. With his kind of money, he could buy his way out of anything. Even now, if he chose to kill her, nothing would be done. *My life would be over, and no one would blink an eye because of who he is. And who I am too.*

Alex raised a brow and looked back toward the prison. It was odd, but he seemed to really be looking at it, with some interest. *Odd.*

"How many inmates does it hold? What are the living conditions?"

It was her turn to be stunned. Alex was asking her questions and really was expecting answers. She knew the facts, but for the life of her, she couldn't understand why he wanted to know.

Ziva provided him those answers, then he came up with more questions. They spent the next hour talking about the prison and the judicial system in Tabiq. Ziva forgot why they were there. It was supposed to be a scare tactic. Instead, it became a history lesson on her country. *I'm not supposed to be enjoying myself, and neither is he. What is wrong with us? This is not a date, yet here we are sitting in the back of a taxi, practically holding hands while debating world politics.*

Ziva called for the taxi driver, and their way back continued with deep, serious, yet engaging, conversations. If this had been an actual date, she'd have considered it one of her better ones. That was sad, considering he was a man she could never allow herself to care about. He was and always would be a Henderson.

As they arrived at the hotel, Ziva pulled herself back onto task. She needed to think logically. If not, she risked him walking her to her room and kissing her goodbye. Neither of those things could happen.

As they exited the taxi, she said, "I have to check in at work. Thank you for accompanying me today. It was . . . interesting."

Alex looked at her as though he was going to stop her. His phone must have vibrated, because he pulled it out from his pocket, checked it, then said, "Have a good night, Ziva."

He left her standing outside the hotel as he made his way back inside. She hoped it wasn't the manager saying the young lady was there, waiting. Whatever the message was, Alex seemed in a rush to respond. *Think positive. He told the manager tomorrow at noon. There's still time. It's not over yet.*

Ziva walked across the street to make it look as though she had a place to be, in case Alex was watching. Today hadn't been a waste of time. She'd learned more about Alex, and she'd provided him with the information she'd set out to. Actually, more than she'd thought possible. Now all she could do was hope he'd contemplate everything she'd said. Her window of opportunity was getting shorter, and her ideas were running low. Tonight would be another sleepless night as she formulated plan B. *And hopefully it won't be haunted by his beautiful eyes or smile. Neither is part of any plan I have.*

Chapter Four

"BRICE CALLED ME twice. When he asked about you, I changed the subject. You should call him."

Bennett could keep his opinion to himself. Although he was marrying into the family, it didn't mean he wanted Brice intruding in his personal business. Brice had left Alex three voicemails while he was out with Ziva yesterday. He wasn't in the mood to retrieve them then and still wasn't now.

The family might be working on interacting with more normalcy, but they were far from their goal. If Brice had called so many times, he was going to use his *eldest* card. It might work with his other siblings, but Alex was immune.

"I have other things on my mind." *Like Ziva, and whatever the hell yesterday was all about.*

He'd enjoyed himself on one of the most outrageous outings he'd ever been on with a woman. She was definitely not like other women. Figuring her out wasn't going to be easy.

"Alex, one of us needs to tell him. I suggest it's you."

He didn't want to hear about what Brice wanted. Alex was more interested in finding out what Bennett learned about Ziva.

"I asked you for information. What did you find?" Alex asked, changing the subject.

"You're making a mistake." He heard Bennett's aggravation in his tone. Alex wasn't about to waste any more time on the phone with him if he had nothing of any importance to say.

"Ziva. Now," Alex barked.

"You spent the day with her and probably have more than I was able to find. This woman has kept herself out of the spotlight."

Alex wished it were the case. They'd spoken for hours, but of nothing personal. "Give me what you have."

"She's twenty-nine years old. Both her parents are deceased. She had an older sister, Isa, but no one would confirm what happened to her. Isa would be a little older than you, if she were alive."

"You think she was . . . abused?" Alex still couldn't bring himself to say the words. The thought of paying for a virgin, an unwilling participant, made him beyond angry. Anyone involved in such acts should be shot. Yet, he was alive because his father came here and did exactly that. He needed to find answers and his mother. Then he had to shut down this fucked-up human trafficking ring for good. For that, he'd need the help of others. *A lot of them.*

"Alex, this is a common theme here. Young women around eighteen disappear, and no one speaks of them again. It's a culture we can't understand. I'm not sure anyone will open up about what is truly going on."

That's why I'm paying for a virgin. My hope is she'll talk to me. Alex knew it wasn't the smartest way to accomplish what he wanted, but it was the easiest. Although the girl would initially be scared shitless, after he explained his true purpose, hopefully she'd help. Maybe she'd have information on her kidnappers . . .

He wondered if Ziva had suffered at the hands of some sick bastard too. She was beautiful, and he could only imagine how valuable she was to them. He held the phone so tightly he thought he'd crush it. If he found out she was assaulted, he'd hunt the asshole down and kill him himself.

"Are you listening, Alex?" Bennett growled in annoyance.

He'd lost track of what Bennett was saying. Alex wasn't going to pretend he'd been listening either. "No. Repeat it."

"I was telling you about Ziva. Both her parents are deceased. There are rumors that as a minor she was sent away to have a baby. Yet, no one ever saw one, and she never spoke of a child to anyone. Somehow she was able to get a job as a secretary in the police department. When I dug deeper, it's more of a file clerk and errand girl. In Tabiq, a married woman cannot work, and single ones rarely get jobs. It isn't as though they're uneducated. They believe a woman's place is in the home, taking care of their husband and children. Since she has neither, she was fortunate to find a place that would hire her. Very few local jobs are considered okay for women."

It didn't sound fortunate to him, and by Bennett's sardonic tone, he knew Bennett felt the same. She'd had a rough life in a horrible country. He still had questions about why she'd followed him when he first arrived. Ziva may be innocent in all this, but yesterday threw him off. Although he enjoyed himself, a ride to the prison wasn't a place he'd expected to go with her. It hadn't been by mistake. She'd intentionally taken him there. *Why?*

"I think she's the one you want to get close to."

"Ziva is staying in the room next to mine. I asked her yesterday if she'd heard any commotion in my room during the break-in. Although she denied it, I know she knows something."

"Do you think she's working with the police to watch you? If so, they know you're not really here for a virgin. You could be in serious danger. We both could. I'll do whatever I have to, but this is no two-man operation."

Bennett was right. It could turn bad quickly. He had a few options. *Let Bennett call in the Turchettas or call Brice.* His gut was telling him he should do neither right now. Once either call was made, they would take control. It didn't mean they wouldn't get results, but the more Alex learned, the more he became personally involved.

"Give me a couple more days to see what I can find out. If things begin to go south, I'll pull this mission."

"Alex, I've been in a lot of rough places. If it turns, you won't have time to reach out for help. It'll be game over. They won't care about your money then."

I don't care about it now. I only want to . . . He was losing focus on his role. First, it was to find his mother. Then stop this nightmare from happening to anyone else. Somewhere along the way he wanted to crush every person who was involved even the slightest. Anger definitely clouded his judgment. It was his choice, his risk, to move forward.

"Bennett, we're in different stages of our lives right now. You have a child on the way and my sister to think about. It might be wise for you to bail now."

"Hell, no. No man left behind. You stay, I stay. Got it?"

Selfish as it may be, he was hoping Bennett felt that way. The chances weren't good, but without Bennett as backup, it was impossible. "Good. Do you think you can pull everything you can about the manager too? We know he's in deep, but we don't know if he's being forced or is doing it out of greed."

"Roger. Can I bring in one more guy? He can be trusted, and for the psychological piece, he'd be the one we need."

"Do I know him?"

"Zoey's met him. Doug Atwood. We served together, and I'd trust him with my life. Hell, I've had to already."

"Make it happen. And make sure your friend keeps his mouth shut. The repercussions if my brothers find out won't be good."

"This guy knows the drill."

Alex knew how much Bennett loved Zoey. If he trusted Doug around her, then he must be all right.

After they disconnected the call, Alex sat and waited. The manager was supposed to deliver his guest at noon. He was not prepared for this. He'd have to wing how to introduce the subject. There weren't any right words to say, and he had no idea what she anticipated would happen. *Yeah. Nothing awkward about this.*

He lay back on the bed, closed his eyes, and tried to focus on anything other than who was about to come knocking on the door. Unfortunately, his mind went to a place not much better. Ziva was still in the adjoining room. How was he going to keep his companion for the night a secret from her? *If she sees the young lady dropped off, there is no way she will believe me, even if I tell her nothing happened. Hell, why would she? She knows I'm James Henderson's son. If I'm even a tenth of the man he was, I'm still a total asshole.*

Alex figured it would be best to approach her ahead of time. He hadn't heard anything from next door, not even her door opening or closing since they returned late last night. *I should check on her. Make sure she's okay.*

It almost made him laugh. He'd never searched for a reason to knock on a woman's door. Yet, here he was, lost for words and trying to come up with an acceptable excuse. He pulled himself off the bed and headed toward the door. Alex didn't need a reason to knock on a door of a room he was paying for. If she didn't like it, she could vacate. *Great. Now I sound like a jerk in my own head.*

Just as he was about to open his door, his phone rang. Pulling it out of his pocket, he saw it was Brice. *Come on. Get the hint. I don't want to talk.*

He declined the call, sending it to voicemail. That didn't stop Brice as he instantly called Alex back. *What the fuck?*

"I hope this is important," Alex barked as he answered the phone.

"Where the hell are you, Alex?"

"On vacation. Since I don't work for you, I don't need your approval to take one," Alex responded snidely.

"Vacation? I don't buy it. Bennett seems to be MIA as well. Is he on *vacation* too?"

Answering for Bennett was a bit more difficult. He didn't care what Brice thought, but whatever he said would most likely make it back to Zoey. He never wanted to hurt her. She'd had enough pain and sadness already, brought on by their father. Choosing his words carefully he said, "I'm not Bennett's keeper either. If you don't have anything important to discuss, I've got someone waiting for me."

"I'm no fool, Alex."

Never thought you were. But if you think you can stop me, you've underestimated me. Just like everyone always has. "Nor am I, Brice."

"You should've talked to me before doing this," Brice said plainly. "There are things you don't know."

"Because you chose not to share them. This isn't the time or the line to do so on." Brice hadn't called the SAT phone and as far as he knew, Brice shouldn't know Alex had one either. *So why the comment about secured lines? Was that a hint you know what I'm really up to?* He wasn't sure how tech savvy these guys were, but he wasn't about to take any chances. There was a lot riding on the next few days. Pissing Brice off was the least of his worries. Doing so might make this look more real if anyone was listening. "Now if you don't mind, I have a sweet young lady who should be arriving soon. We can finish this when I return to the States."

Alex hung up the phone and slipped it in his pocket. He knew Brice was going to be ripping mad. Sure enough, his phone vibrated again. He didn't need to look. Brice, if anything, was persistent. *Stubborn runs in our genes. He may as well wake up and realize I'm in charge of my own life. I have been for a very long time.*

He reached for the doorknob one more time. When he opened it, there was a young woman standing shyly on the other side. She was so tiny and fragile looking. They had her wearing a delicate white dress, surely not a mistake. She definitely looked the innocent virgin, and she was being forced to go to him.

He couldn't imagine what must be going through her mind. No matter how sheltered she may have been, this would be horrifying for her. *Don't worry, little one.*

It's not what you think. Not what any of them think. He wished he could tell her he wasn't going to touch her or hurt her in any way.

Out of the corner of his eye, he saw a large man at the end of the hallway, watching the interaction. If Alex did or said something now to ease her mind, it might be a red flag that something was off. No matter how his heart ached for the young girl's predicament, he couldn't afford for this to look like anything other than him paying for a sexual service. One wrong move and he knew all hell would break out.

Alex hated it, but he needed the man down the hall to report back that all was okay. Reaching out, he brushed some of her long dark hair from her face. She didn't budge but squeezed her eyes shut. With her no longer looking at him, Alex gave the guy what he needed. *My approval for the product.* "Nice. Very nice."

He hoped that was enough, because scaring this child any more didn't sit well with him. *I'd rather take a bullet than hurt her.*

Alex needed them out of sight. Reaching out a hand, he took hers gently. Her hand was shaking as he held it. It was like a punch in his gut, but he needed to push forward.

"Come in." He led her inside and shut the door behind them.

Once inside, he walked her over to the couch, let go of her hand, and said, "Please sit down." With trembling legs, she did as he asked. He was going to sit too, but he needed a few minutes. Alex had rehearsed what he was going to say over and over. With her here in front of him, his words didn't seem to be enough. *Why should she believe me?*

He had to try. He'd come this far. Letting her leave without going through with what he'd paid for wasn't an option because they would know this had all been a sham. He needed to find a way to make every disgusting thing look as though it happened, without even touching this girl. *It's not just me who needs to be a good liar. I'm banking on someone who doesn't know me from a hole in the wall.* And that's when he realized there was a large hole in his plan. If he wasn't able to stop the assholes involved in the ring, what would happen to the girl before him? Either way, he was condemning her life. She'd be ostracized from her family and put on the streets. How would he protect her? Could he protect her? *Shit. What do I do with her?*

He took a deep breath and sat down across from her. "Do you speak English?"

The girl nodded. *That's a start. I don't know what I would do if she didn't. It sure as hell would've been a short conversation.* From what Alex had observed, most people in Tabiq spoke their language and English when they chose to.

"My name is, Alex. What's yours?"

"Myla," she said, looking down at the floor, and her hands folded tightly in her lap.

"I'm not going to hurt you."

She didn't look up, but he noticed her flinch. *Of course, that's a line that most women have heard, right before the creep hurts them.*

"I only want to talk. Will you talk to me?"

Myla tensed even more but nodded.

"How old are you?"

"Eighteen." Her voice was barely a whisper as she answered.

At least she's legal. Just not a willing participant. "Did they tell you why you're here?"

Myla nodded again. Alex could see her lip quiver and tears pool in her eyes. He was trying to ease into the conversation. Maybe that was the wrong approach. Going too quickly might scare the shit out of her. *Can it really get any worse? She knows why she's here, only waiting for me to pounce. Anything has to be better than that.*

So much flew through Alex's mind. He wasn't sure what to tell her. He needed her to stay with him for the entire duration. If she decided to bolt, it'd bring questions. Questions he couldn't and didn't want to answer. Tying her down and gagging her was out of the question. She wasn't his prisoner. She was already traumatized when she was ripped from her own family. He needed to do something very difficult for him. *I'm going to have to trust in someone I don't know.*

The worst thing would be if she didn't listen and ran out of the room, heading straight to the hotel manager and told him everything. Alex's only recourse would be to call Bennett and have him come in shooting. *Take out a few of the bastards along the way. Of course, that was a plan fraught with holes.*

Alex wished he knew something about her. It'd give him an edge to work with. Instead, he was going in blind. *If I can pull this off, it sure as hell will make one fucking amazing research story for my next book, if nothing else. But damn, I'm hoping for more than that. I'm going for it all. I want this ring shut down, and I want to find my mother. I'm not exactly sure what I want to tell her, but I want her to know I'm sorry. Sorry for any brutality she experienced at the hands of my father. To make life easier for her if there is a way I can. I want to pay for the debt she's carried.*

It was time to go big or go home as they say. *Here goes nothing.* "I'm going to tell you some things, and I need you to trust me. If you don't, it's going to be very dangerous for both of us. Do you understand?"

Myla nodded, but he wasn't sure she grasped what he was trying to say to her. "I trust you." Her body language said differently.

"Do you know who I am?"

"Yes."

"And do you know who my father was?"

Alex watched a tear rolled down Myla's cheek. "Yes."

It should surprise him that someone so young would know who James Henderson was. It had been thirty years since his father had come here. Unfortunately that was based on the birthdate of his youngest sibling. His father's travels documented that it should've been. *One can hide a lot for the right price.* What had allured him still existed here, so it was possible he continued to visit. *If he did, could there be more children we don't know about? Damn, the questions are endless, and the answers nil.* He could only imagine what his father may have done to leave such a lasting impression. *Even through the generations. How many women suffered at his hands? How many families were ripped apart due to his greed?*

He reached out to the tissue box on the coffee table and pulled out a Kleenex. He hoped he wouldn't require one for himself. Just thinking of what his father had done here shook him to the core. Handing the Kleenex to Myla he said, "I'm not my father."

"No. You're his son," Myla said, her voice filled with contempt.

One of them. It was apparent she didn't understand what he was trying to tell her. "I am his son, but I do not act like he did. Or treat people the way he did." Alex knew it was going to take a hell of a lot more than just words to convince her. Understandably, he was being judged by his father's actions, which had been the same throughout their lives.

Myla looked up and met his eyes. "I don't understand."

He was going to try his best to explain the difference, without detailing what they both already knew about his father. They were words Alex couldn't verbalize. He had no idea how someone as young as Myla comprehended such horrific acts. *It's sad that it's a lifestyle she doesn't believe she can fight against. I'm here to end that, hopefully.* "James Henderson was a very evil man, and he hurt a lot of people." *Even his own children.* "I don't hurt people." *Or try not to.*

She looked confused. "But you had them bring me here when I didn't want to come. That is hurting someone. Hurting me."

"Yes, I did. I needed you here so they would . . . think I'm like my father."

"Everyone thinks you're like him."

He'd felt that from the moment he disembarked from the plane. "I know. I want them to think that."

"Why would you want people to think that you're . . . evil?"

Sounds crazy even coming from you. "So they would send you to me."

Myla got up off the couch and started to pace. He could see her looking around the room, hoping to find an escape. Alex couldn't let her leave. Not yet. *Not until the week I've paid for is over.*

Alex reached out and took hold of her arm. "You can't leave, Myla."

"You lied. You are going to hurt me. I knew it. I knew it," Myla whimpered. Tears poured down her cheeks, and she shook with fear. Her voice became louder, but just above a whisper. "You're hurting me. You're hurting me!"

He hadn't realized how tightly he'd gripped her small arm. Letting her arm go, she slipped to her side, but he could see the red spots where his fingers once were. "I'm very sorry."

Myla brought a hand up to rub where his hand had left its mark.

In a much softer voice, Alex tried to calm her. "Please, Myla. I need your help. If you can trust me, I'll show you I don't mean you harm."

"Why should I believe you? You're a Henderson. I know why you're here."

"No. You know why my father came here. That is not why I came."

"Then why are you here?"

His other family didn't know, yet here he was about to open up to someone he'd met only minutes before. They shared something. *We're both knee-deep in this, and we both need someone to trust.* He hoped she could shed some light on what happened to the other women of Tabiq who had faced what their mothers had. It was obvious this was an ongoing practice. He wasn't sure if it was for the same reason his father came. *Children. Unwanted or not.* No matter what the reason for the others, it had to stop. *To stop it, you have to know what you're dealing with. For that I need someone on the inside who's willing to speak the truth.* Alex wasn't sure if it was foolish betting on Myla, but his options were limited.

"My mother is from here. I'm here to find her and to put a stop to all this . . . this abuse that is happening to girls like you." *And like my mother.*

"Your mother lives here? Who is she?" Myla asked,

her eyes getting as big as saucers.

"I don't know. It's what I need to find out. I need you to help me, and trust me. If you do, I promise to help you and your family so no harm will come to any of you again."

Myla looked at him, meeting him square in the eyes. "So my sisters will not be sold like me?"

His heart was ripping apart as he saw the pain in this young girl's eyes. She was well aware of what was expected of her and the others. "I promise you, Myla. No one will hurt them. I'll make sure of it. Will you do as I ask?"

She nodded. "For my sisters, I'll do as you ask."

"Good. First, you must promise not to tell anyone about this. It appears no one here can be trusted, maybe a few can be, but they're afraid to take a stand against this. Everyone must think you've provided the services I paid for."

"They'll think I'm . . . tarnished."

"Only for now. Once this is done, we can tell them the truth. For now, no one must know." He could see she was torn about making such a promise. "This is only until I have the information I need. Then the truth will come out."

"Okay. I will not tell anyone, and I'll help you so we can stop this evil from happening."

"Good. I'm counting on you." Originally, he'd had the adjoining room set aside for Myla. But it was occupied by Ziva. Although he liked having her close by, it made the sleeping arrangements more difficult with Myla. On the positive side, it also meant she couldn't slip out during the night, without him noticing. *Thank God, I'm a light sleeper.* "There is only one bed. I'll take the couch. If for any reason housekeeping or room service comes in, we must make it look as though we share the bed. Understood?"

Myla looked toward the bed then back to Alex. Her eyes were wide with concern. "And you'll not come in the bed with me there?" Her voice shook slightly when she asked.

"No, Myla. I will not touch you in any way to hurt you. I'll stay on the couch. If anyone does see us together, we'll have to make it look like you and I have had relations."

"Relations?"

Damn it. "Sex." Alex wasn't shy about such things, but saying it to someone who was half his age, disturbed him.

"What will you do?"

"I will not take it too far. Maybe put an arm around your waist or hold your hand. Trust me, Myla, we are *not* having sex. This is strictly for show. We'll pretend."

Myla seemed to have calmed down and headed to the couch. "If anyone comes in, I will help make it look real, as long as you promise that it's not. What happens if they do not believe us?"

"You know Tabiq better than I do. I'm sure they'll not be happy."

Her eyes darkened with sadness. Her voice sounded as though she was about to cry again. "They will put me to death. You? I'm not sure. You are rich, and they will not want to lose your money, but they'll not be happy. Lying to them is a very bad and dangerous thing to do."

He didn't want her life at risk like that. Maybe he could set her free now before it went any further and try to find another way. *If there was one, I'd have taken it already. If I stop now, I better be on the next flight out of Tabiq.*

"Don't worry about me, Myla. If you do just as I tell you, we both will make it out of here alive."

Myla yawned, and he could tell she was worn out from her ordeal.

"Would you like to rest?"

She nodded and headed for the couch. He raised a hand and pointed to the large king-sized bed. For the first time since he'd opened the door, Myla smiled. "May I use the bathroom?"

Alex was relieved she'd relaxed somewhat. *This entire ordeal must be scary as fuck. The fact you're willing to trust me even a little blows my mind. No time to question it.*

"Yes, of course. I placed pajamas on the bureau for you to change into. I didn't know what size to bring, but hopefully they won't be too large on you."

Myla tensed up again. She walked to the bureau, picked up the pajamas and held them up. Her smile returned when she saw his choice. They were modest and not sexy in the least.

Turning back to face him she said, "Thank you, Alex. I have heard so many stories about your father and feared my fate would be the same as the others. The thought of meeting you had me shaking with fear. I won't lie. I'm still afraid."

"That's perfectly understandable. If you weren't, you'd be foolish. I'm a stranger, and all I can give you is my word. Give me time, and I'll prove that you can trust me." After all these people had been through, trust was going to be a hard thing to earn, if not impossible.

"My options are limited. My life was in your hands the moment you answered the door, and I hope I am wise to do so, but I'll trust in your word."

Alex nodded, and she headed off to the bathroom with her pajamas in hand. This was the first step, a very small one, but he knew it wasn't going to be easy. What he hadn't expected was how emotionally difficult this was going to be on him as well. Myla was barely eighteen. If it had not been him, he knew they would've sold her to another man, and her safety and innocence wouldn't exist any longer. *As long as I'm here, no one will hurt her.*

While she was in the bathroom, Alex pulled on a clean white T-shirt. Normally he slept in his boxer shorts, but fully clothed was the way to go while she was in his room.

After she finished in the bathroom, she went to the bed, pulled down the covers, and climbed in. He turned away before she pulled the blankets up around her.

Alex went back to the couch and lay down. He looked over at her several times, and she was lying wide awake, gripping the sheet tightly around her neck. Alex wanted to reassure her he wouldn't hurt her. Words were simple; actions were all that mattered. He wasn't sure if she was going to get any sleep.

He was exhausted himself; last night he'd tortured himself over this meeting. Now with the initial contact out of the way, he had to plan out phase two. *We've got a long way to go before I can get the people in charge of this ring to trust me. All I can do for the moment is hope I can keep Myla believing in what I have said, with no proof to offer as validation.*

A few hours after tossing and turning ideas around in his head, he heard a noise from the other side of the room. Looking over the back of the couch again, he saw Myla sound asleep and snoring. Asleep, she looked younger than she said. Her situation sickened him, but for now, Myla was under his protection. He'd given her his word, and if it was the last thing he'd do, he'd ensure she and her family were safe.

Myla rolled over and hugged the pillow. No matter what his stress level was, he couldn't imagine what it'd been for her last night, thinking about what was to transpire today. He felt good right now. It wasn't much, but he'd saved one. Or at least, he was trying to ensure she didn't become a statistic like so many before her.

Rest now, little one. This week is going to be long and tense for the both of us.

ZIVA'S HEART SANK. She'd honestly hoped that Alex had heard what she was saying yesterday and would've changed his mind. Knowing he wasn't strong enough to resist was disappointing, to say the least. So many men had come before him, yet Alex was different. She'd seen something in him, something she believed was good and honorable. *I was foolish and only saw what I wanted to see. He's just like his father, and I can't forget that.*

Even though she'd hoped he wouldn't do anything, Ziva had been hanging close by her bedroom door, waiting for the slightest sound. When she heard the woman's footsteps she knew one thing, Alex was about to get his visitor.

Ziva had opened her door the slightest crack to peer at the girl. She was maybe eighteen, but not a day older. And the white dress of innocence made her look even younger. When Ziva saw Alex reach out and take the girl by the hand and lead her into his room, she barely controlled herself. All she wanted to do was fling open her door, go up in his face and tell him what a lousy piece of shit he was, and he truly was no different than his father.

The only thing that prevented her taking immediate action was her understanding of how these things went down. The girls were never let out of sight until they were in the room. That meant someone had been watching. Ziva couldn't have risked being noticed as well. If she'd been spotted spying on Alex and the girl, never mind trying to intervene, the manager would've turned her over to the authorities. She couldn't do any good if she was six feet underground.

Ziva felt so helpless with the whole situation, as she had on so many occasions, living in Tabiq. She hurt for the young girl next door and for the girl's family. She knew the grief they would experience. All she could do was lie on her bed and cry herself to sleep. She'd been so close yet still unable to prevent the act from happening. She'd told herself so many times if she died saving at least one, she'd given her life for a worthy cause.

Instead, she was in the room next to theirs, trying not to imagine what was taking place. Ziva put a pillow over her head so no sound would penetrate. She was angry with herself. This was her chance, and she'd blown it. *I failed her. I'm sorry, whoever you are. I wanted to do something, but I wasn't brave enough.*

Tears rolled down her face, and her sobs muffled under the pillow. She wasn't going to give up. She may not have been able to stop Alexander Henderson today, but she wasn't going to give up. Somehow Ziva was going to get the girl alone and get her out of that room and the hotel. She'd take her to the one place she knew was still safe. The place her father had taken her all those years ago. If the government never found it, she knew Alexander wouldn't either. She might not have been able to prevent it, but she was going to cut it short.

Ziva needed to let the pain of what happened go. Holding on to it would only interfere with her pulling off the next step. She needed to be on top of her game.

Brushing the tears from her face, she thought how to get the girl alone. The only thing she could think of was to knock on Alex's door and invite him to come to her room. *That's not going to save the girl but maybe buy her enough time to escape. If she gets free, maybe I can help her. As long as no one else finds her first. How would the girl know where to go?*

Ziva let out a heavy sigh. It wasn't much, but she had a plan. First thing tomorrow she'd knock on that door. Until then, she'd close her eyes and pray for sleep, because tomorrow she needed to be rested and ready to go. *With Alex, I can't guarantee how anything is going to go. Yesterday I would've bet he would've sent the girl away. So wrong. I won't underestimate him again.* She'd never forget who he was. *A Henderson.*

Chapter Five

ALEX COULDN'T TALK to Bennett in front of Myla. He was willing to put himself on the line, but he wouldn't risk putting Bennett in more danger. So far no one had made the connection, and he was going to keep it that way.

Slipping out of the room while Myla slept, Alex left the hotel and headed across the street. He could still keep an eye on the hotel but was far enough away not to be overheard.

He pulled out his SAT phone and called Bennett. "Need you to pull more information."

"Roger."

He proceeded to give him Myla's information.

"That's not a lot to go on, Alex."

"It's all I have. People aren't forthcoming on information. I'm sure you can guess why."

"From what I found out about the manager, I can see why this town is so fucked up. That bastard is in deep with this shit. He's pulling all the strings *here*, but is just a puppet to the ringmaster."

"You're telling me if we take him out, this shuts down today?"

"No. He'd be replaced. We need to get to him so we can get to his boss. Then we're making headway. Until then, it's not going to have any long-term effect."

Alex hated waiting, yet trusting Bennett's judgment was his only choice. He was only one person, and he'd never make it out the front door of the hotel if he acted irrationally. Besides, he needed to start the ball rolling on Myla's family. If they acted before the family was out and safe, they most likely would pay the price. He wouldn't let that happen.

"You keep track of every move that bastard makes. I want him out as soon as we can. First I need that information on Myla."

"What are you going to do?"

"I made promises I plan on keeping." He didn't feel the need to share the details with Bennett. This secret was between Myla and himself. *I wish I could do more.*

"Don't do anything stupid," Bennett barked over the phone.

"You handle your end, and let me worry about mine," Alex snapped back.

"Famous last words from someone when they're about to fuck up."

Alex disconnected the call. He wouldn't argue that point. If Brice were here instead of him, things would be going like clockwork. *But if Brice was in charge, they'd still be in the States and who'd be protecting Myla?*

Somehow his gut told him Ziva would. She was keeping her distance from him, yet he knew she wasn't far away. It was weird, but he sensed her watching him. It wasn't in a sexual way either. But he wasn't sure if she was out to protect him or take him down. Ordinarily, he could read women clearly, but Ziva was entirely different. From the moment he spotted her, she'd been a mystery. If it were any other place or time, he would've taken on the challenge of unraveling the layers she had cocooned around her. He found her utterly intriguing.

Unfortunately, the last thing he needed was another person to be involved in this mess. Bringing her any closer to him than he already had might put her life at risk as well. *I'm not willing to do that. For her own good, I need to stay away from her. Once I let Myla into my room, I became a man Ziva should run from. Even though it's a façade, there are people who won't believe or forget it.*

He knew Ziva was far more observant than she pretended to be and probably heard or saw Myla entering his room. Whatever connection he thought they might have shared would've vanished and have been replaced with hatred. In her eyes, Alex was another sick bastard taking advantage of a young, innocent girl. Ordinarily, he didn't care what anyone thought of him, but for some reason, Ziva was different. It was troubling him. That didn't mean he could knock on her door and tell her the truth. She worked for the police department. The less she knew about him and the real reason he was there, the better for her. *I'd rather read the disdain in your eyes now than the desire I believe I saw when you took me on our little expedition.*

There were difficult choices to make, but he needed to protect Ziva. If he told her the truth, she'd be all-in and ready to help. That would put her life at risk too. There was no need to do so. She was safe right now, and he would do anything he had to for that to continue. *Even if that means making her hate me. As long as she lives through this fucking mess, it'll be worth it.*

As Alex made his way back to the hotel, he looked to the floor where their rooms were. He could see the light turned on in Ziva's room. *What are you up to?* Something felt off. He needed to get back there quickly. Even though he'd told Myla not to speak to anyone, Ziva could be very convincing. *I'm the proof. She took me with her for an entire day, when I had no intention of going. I can only imagine the power she'd have with a naïve kid.*

When he entered the foyer, the manager called out to him. "Is everything okay, Mr. Henderson?"

"Fine," Alex barked. His gut said otherwise. *Let me be wrong.*

He didn't wait for the elevator and decided to bolt up the three flights of stairs instead. As soon as he came around the corner, he stopped and looked down the hallway. Everything was as quiet as it had been when he'd left earlier. Until he was inside and saw Myla was unharmed, he wouldn't be satisfied.

Alex stopped outside of Ziva's door, pressed his ear against it, and listened to see if he could hear her moving around. All was silent. With the lights on, he knew she was awake. *What are you up to, young lady?*

Even though he told himself he wouldn't do it, he knocked gently on her door and waited. No answer. He tried the door, and it was locked. Alex had the spare key in his room, and after checking on Myla, he was going to head back there and check on Ziva.

Going to his room next door, he inserted the key and opened the door. When he went inside, he saw the bed was unmade and empty. He looked around the room and realized the door adjoining his and Ziva's room was open. *Shit!* He bolted over, and to his dismay, her room was vacant as well. *Damn! Damn! Damn!*

He'd been foolish to leave either of them alone, even for a short time. Looking around, he saw no sign of struggle, which meant they'd left willingly. *Why? They were safe here. Now they have no one to protect them.*

Pulling his phone out of his pocket, he called Bennett.

"They're gone!"

"Who?

"Ziva and Myla. They're both gone," Alex barked into the phone. His heart was racing as he thought what would happen to them if they were caught. "Get over here now. We need to find them."

"No one knows our connection. Keep it that way, Alex. If they put two and two together, we lose the upper hand, not that we had much of one to start with. It's the only card we have in our pocket."

His mind was racing. Alex hadn't anticipated someone coming in and taking them. If he had, he'd never have left them. In hindsight, it was a mistake he hoped those two ladies didn't pay for. *I'll never forgive myself if anything happens to them.*

Alex needed to do something, but he had no idea where to start looking. "How the hell are we going to find them, Bennett? No one here is going to give us any information."

"Tracking is one of my specialties. I need you to sit tight. Whatever you do, don't let anyone know they're gone."

Alex remembered the manager trying to talk to him when he arrived. *Had he seen them being taken? Is he the one who took them?* If he found out the girls were harmed, he'd kill the bastard.

"You can't expect me to—"

"Do you want to find them alive?" Bennett snapped.

It was a stupid question. Bennett was lucky this conversation was taking place on the phone, because if it was in person, Alex would've laid him out on his ass. His back was up against a wall as to what his next steps would be. If he made the wrong move, everything he'd set out to accomplish would be over, but even worse, he'd be risking Ziva's life. Alex had to put his pride on the back burner for the moment. "That's why I want to help."

"This is what I do, Alex. I'll find them. Once I have a visual, I'll be in contact. Until then, don't leave your room, and speak to no one. Remember, you're being watched, even if you don't see them."

"Bennett, you were here before. What makes you think they aren't keeping an eye on you?"

"I know they are. The first time I came, I made myself very unpopular. The ringleaders are keeping their distance from me on purpose. They suspect I'm here looking to shut down shit. They, on the other hand, think you're just a piece of shit. See the difference?"

Yeah. Unfortunately, I do. "Then give them something to confirm their beliefs."

"Roger that. I'm going to find those girls, and I'm not going to be quiet about it when I do."

"I don't care as long as they don't get hurt." Alex had made a promise to Myla, and he'd keep it, but he couldn't get Ziva's face and smile out of his mind. He needed to see it again. His best bet at doing so was trusting Bennett. *Don't let me down.*

ZIVA GRIPPED THE steering wheel tightly and continued to look in her mirrors, making sure they weren't being followed. This journey was one she'd made once a week and had for many years.

Peering into the backseat, she said, "It's okay, Myla, we're almost there."

"I'm scared," Myla replied, her voice cracking.

"I know you are. But once we're there, you'll be safe. No one can hurt you there." *Not even the rich and powerful Alex Henderson.*

"What about my family? He said he'd—" Myla cut herself off, and Ziva could only imagine what Alex had said.

That bastard threatened your family? God, how cruel can he be? Ziva was getting a pretty good picture of how sick he was. All her hope for him was gone. Just looking at Myla now and seeing the fear in her eyes broke her heart. Ziva didn't want to think of the horrible things Alex had done to this poor girl. *But I promise you, Alex, you're not going to get away with it.*

"Nothing will happen to your family, Myla. I promise you that."

They were almost there, and Ziva turned off the road. Parking behind trees, they needed to make the rest of the way on foot. The brush had grown very high since her father had hidden her away here. Cutting it back wasn't an option, at times it had become even scarier than it had been before. *Hard to believe because things were so bad when I was a child. I never thought it could get worse, but it has. Add drugs on top of the selling of virgins, and we are the lowest place to visit, never mind raise a family.*

Ziva had the opportunity to leave Tabiq years ago. She couldn't bring herself to do it. Even though she no longer had any family here, it was still her home, the place of her birth. If there were any chance, even a small one of making Tabiq a better place, she'd stay and try.

"We're almost there," Ziva said, glancing at Myla.

"Where are we going?"

"A place I stayed when I was young." *A place I still come to regularly.*

"You mean so no one took you?" Myla asked.

"Yes." It was sad so many girls understood their fate and had no choice but to accept it. Most of them were used for a night or two then sent back to their families. It was only James Henderson who flew the women out of Tabiq and returned months later. No one knew what or where they'd been taken. *Everyone was too scared to ask, and the girls knew better than to say.* Ziva had to make Myla understand how lucky she was. If she hadn't been there to stop Alexander, Myla could be on her way to God knows where by now.

When they came to the cabin, everything looked quiet and abandoned. She stopped at the edge of the clearing and listened. She could hear the wind blowing through the surrounding trees but nothing else. *Just the way it should be.*

Myla ran up from behind Ziva and took hold of her hand. She gave it a light supportive squeeze. "You're going to like it here. It's very . . . peaceful."

When she was here it was also lonely, as no one came by except her father to bring supplies. That wasn't the case now. The cabin appeared to be vacant, but it was far from the truth. There were five young girls hidden away inside. They were all younger than Myla so they hadn't yet experienced what she had. Yet, they all shared similar fears.

Stopping outside the cabin, she turned to Myla and

said, "You'll find girls here who also are away from their families. They have not suffered . . . at the hands of a man like Mr. Henderson, but they also can't leave this hiding place, or they will. You must not ever leave or tell another living soul about it. If you do, your fate will also become theirs. Do you understand?"

Myla looked at the cabin then back to Ziva. "You mean they are all still . . ."

"Innocent?" Myla nodded. "Yes, they are. Help me so we can keep them that way."

"How old are they?" Myla asked.

"The youngest is fourteen and the oldest sixteen. In a few years, they'll be of age to . . . to be taken."

Myla looked at Ziva questioningly. "You do this? Help protect girls from being sold?"

Ziva nodded. "I try. There are only a few here, and so many more girls I couldn't help."

"But you're helping some. That is the beginning, Ziva. You know what they'll do to you if you get caught?"

Ziva knew all too well. It was a risk worth taking as far as she was concerned. "I do."

Myla pulled herself up tall and said confidently, "I want to be part of that. I want to help too. Just like you."

"Thank you, Myla. You can help. These girls need someone to look after them. To look up to. You can be that for them."

"I would like that. But what about Mr. Henderson?"

"He won't find you here. No one will."

"He'll worry what happened to me. I promised him I

wouldn't leave, and I broke my word."

Ziva didn't understand why Myla was so concerned about Alexander. He seemed to have her so scared; she had misplaced loyalty to him. After a few days of seeing he couldn't hurt her any longer, she'd settle down and change that worry into anger or hate. *Emotions she really should be displaying.* She wasn't a psychologist so she could only go on how she'd feel if Alexander had taken her by force. *There's no way in hell I would be defending him. Stringing him up by his balls, yes, defending, no.* All Ziva could do was be there for Myla when she did break.

It hadn't been easy gaining the trust of even the girls she had. Convincing them to trust her and leave their parents was no small feat, but she had. Ziva had to believe she'd be able to reach Myla too. *She came with me here. That's a start.*

"Can you please do me a favor?" Myla asked.

"Of course. What do you need?" Ziva would do anything she could to help Myla through this difficult time.

"I need you to go back to the hotel and tell Mr. Henderson I'm sorry."

Ziva almost jumped out of her skin. Myla was in worse shape than she thought. "You do *not* owe him anything, Myla. What he's done is wrong. Whatever he told you to make you think you deserved to be treated in such a manner is a lie. He had absolutely no right to take advantage of you as he did."

Ziva hadn't meant for her voice to rise as it had, but she was angry for Myla. She had every intention of going back to the hotel, but it sure wasn't going to be to apologize to that bastard.

The cabin door opened and the other girls came out to see what the shouting was about. Ziva turned to see some of them about to burst into tears. All this time, she'd come and held things together. Things seemed out of control.

Taking a deep breath, she said in a calmer tone, "It's okay. I'm not angry at Myla. I'm just angry at someone else who . . . disappointed me. Don't worry. You're okay here. He won't come."

Only then did they begin to settle down. Slowly, one by one, the girls came over to stand by her. "This is Myla. She's going to be staying with you now. When I'm not here, she's in charge, so you need to listen to what she says."

"Myla, my name is Cali. Do you know how to read?"

Myla smiled. "Yes, I do. My father taught me. Do you know how?"

Cali shook her head. "No. I had no father, and my mother didn't know how. Can you teach me?"

Myla reached out, took Cali by the hand, and headed into the cabin. "Why don't we go inside and start right away?"

The other girls grabbed the supplies Ziva had brought and helped carry them inside. Ziva stood there, looking at the cabin. What was once a place she hated, now was one of hope, and at times like this, even joy. *Thank you, Papa. Thanks for giving me a chance to carry on what you started.*

Chapter Six

"No one has seen them? That's impossible. Myla is young, and they might be able to get her to go with them quietly, but Ziva? She'd have gone down kicking and screaming." *She might be tiny, but damn she's no pushover.*

"I agree with you. That leaves only one scenario," Bennett said.

"Which is?"

"Ziva took Myla."

Alex wouldn't lie. That had crossed his mind, but only briefly. Ziva never would've risked Myla's life like that. "That doesn't make any sense. Ziva knows if Myla is caught running away, she could be put to death. Why would she take her?"

"Simple. Ziva is trying to protect Myla from *you*."

Me? Oh, God. "She thinks I really—"

"I'd say so, since they're both gone. Now, all we need to do is find out where Ziva would feel safe enough that she'd take Myla. Everything I found out about her so far says she's a gentle, caring soul."

You weren't out on our date. She talked about prisons and death sentences. Or maybe she just saves that kind of talk for me. The me she believes deserves it. "Did you find out where she lives?"

"Yes, and she's not there. I even found her family home. No one has been there in years."

"Any friends or family?" There had to be someone who knew more about her than he did.

"She keeps to herself when she's not working. I can guarantee she didn't take Myla to the police station. That department is so deep in this mess; she'd have been a fool to go there."

That puzzled Alex. *Why work there if they're so bad?* Ziva became more complex as each moment passed. She was charming and beautiful, so being alone had to be a choice. Lack of friends also a choice. Working for the lion's den is what threw him. Surely there were other options for employment.

"Bennett, what exactly did she have access to at the police department?"

"Records."

That gave her the perfect place to gather information on what was happening. *And how she'd known I was here. It would explain why she followed me from the airport. She knew who I was from the beginning.*

"Are you sure she's not something more for them?"

"Like what?"

"A detective."

Bennett laughed. "From what you told me about her,

she's no detective or spy."

"I may have been wrong. Thinking back, I might've been a bit distracted to have noticed a few things."

"Great. We're here in a hostile country with our lives on the line, and you're too busy to notice if the person in the next room is friend or foe?"

Alex could hear the anger in Bennett's voice, but it didn't bother him. There were bigger things on his mind. *I need to know they're both safe.*

"Bennett, you do a hell of a lot of bragging, so it's time to deliver. I want to know where they are within the next twelve hours."

Bennett laughed. "I don't remember being on your payroll. You'll have your answers. I'm just not sure you'll like them."

The call disconnected. Alex knew he'd pushed Bennett's buttons. He needed to remind himself he wasn't some hired guy. Bennett was going to be his brother-in-law, the father of his soon-to-be nephew or niece. For as much as he pushed, he had to ensure Bennett made it back to Boston, back to Zoey, safe and sound. *He's not any more expendable than Ziva or Myla. Not in Zoey's eyes, and I can't forget that.*

Bennett could handle himself in any situation. If things became too hot, he'd bypass Alex in a heartbeat and call for backup. That knowledge should piss him off, yet Alex knew it wasn't just his own ass he was protecting if Bennett made such a call.

The room phone rang. Alex was tempted to ignore it

but doing so might bring a knock on the door instead.

Picking up the receiver, he said, "Henderson here."

"Mr. Henderson. I'm checking to see if your delivery was to your liking?" the manager asked.

Alex couldn't believe the audacity the guy had to check on such a thing. They literally treated the women here with no worth, except for the good old-fashioned dollar they brought in. *I'm going to enjoy bringing your ass down.*

"Everything is fine. I'd prefer we not be disturbed again. Do I make myself clear?"

"Extremely. Sorry for the interruption. Good day."

Alex hung up. It would buy him some time, but he was sure housekeeping would want to come in, and there also was room service for food. *Shit. They are going to expect us to eat.*

Immediately Alex rang down and placed an order for two. "We will be occupied, so please knock and leave the cart outside the door."

"Yes, sir."

He took a quick shower as the heat of the day was already here. When he returned, he hoped the food had arrived. He was starving but would settle for a cup of coffee. The day was half over and off to a rough start. It seemed like it wasn't going to change anytime soon, so he might as well rest up for the fight he knew was coming. There was a single knock on his door. Wrapped in only a towel, he went over and opened it. Sure enough, the rolling table set for two sat outside his door.

Alex opened the door wide and dragged the cart inside. Then he locked the door again and slipped the chain across the top. It wouldn't stop anyone for long, but if things went south, it might buy him a few seconds.

He was just about to sit down and eat when he heard the door in the next room open and close. *Fuck. I didn't shut the adjoining room door.* He grabbed the only thing he could think of, a table knife, and headed for the other room. *Whoever you are, if you're not packing then you're done.*

Entering the room with the knife clearly displayed in front of him, he stopped abruptly as Ziva gasped only inches away.

"What the hell do you think you're doing?" she asked.

He grabbed her arm and pulled her close, never letting the knife drop. "I should ask you the same thing. Where is Myla?"

Ziva held her head up high and said, "Someplace you'll never find her."

Alex was torn between relieved to see Ziva and wanting to wring her pretty little neck. "You had no right to take her from here. Do you know the danger she's in now?"

Ziva laughed. "Less than with you."

He lowered the knife and tossed it onto her bed. Then he let go of her. Alex ran his hand through his hair and said, "You don't know anything about what's going on, Ziva."

"I know you're a Henderson. I know what you did to the poor child. There isn't anything more I care to know. What you don't seem to realize is I'm not going to let you get away with it."

Alex looked down at her. Ziva meant exactly what she was saying. He had to give her credit, she could act tough, but that's all it was. It wouldn't get her far. If he weren't really one of the good guys, she'd have found that out already.

"You're not in any position to stop me from anything I choose to do."

Alex regretted the words once they left his mouth. Ziva now a few feet away from him, reached behind her back and pulled out a gun. With it pointed square at his bare chest she said, "On the contrary, Mr. Henderson, you're in no position to stop me."

ZIVA'S HEART WAS pounding in her chest. She'd never threatened anyone in her life, never held a gun. Here she was with a loaded weapon leveled on Alex, a man she once dreamt about kissing. Now all she wanted to do was kiss his ass goodbye.

Her fingers trembled, holding the butt of the gun, and she had to remind herself what he'd done to Myla. If she didn't stop him, Alex would just move on to the next girl, and the next after that, just like his father had.

"Put the gun down, Ziva."

"Since you just had a knife pointed at me, I don't think that'd be wise. And if you haven't figured it out,

I'm no fool," she snarled at him. Ziva hated that, even with a gun in her hand and Alex wrapped only in a towel, she still found him intimidating. It wasn't going to be easy to pull this off, but she had to try. "Now get dressed. You're coming with me."

Alex didn't move. "Where are we going?"

"Don't ask questions. Just do as you're told," Ziva said in a demanding tone that almost sounded authentic.

Alex nodded and turned back toward his room. She followed close behind him, never lowering the gun. Once inside his room, they walked to his closet. Ziva didn't want to look, but his body . . . He was solid muscle from head to toe. *At least, with your back to me, I don't have to worry about you catching me looking.*

Of course, those beautiful muscles turned out to be a distraction with a high price to pay. Alex took a step forward, and at the same time he brought his left arm backward, pushing the gun away from him. He spun around so fast and grabbed hold of her wrist that she had no choice but to release the weapon to him.

Tears clouded her vision. The girls . . . How would she protect the girls who would be left without a silent advocate in their corner?

Ziva lowered her head in defeat, and her entire body went limp. Alex, now with the gun in his hand, swooped her up against his bare chest with the free hand.

"It's okay. I have you." His voice was soft and consoling.

Ziva was full of anguish and pain. She didn't want to

give in. She'd worked so hard, stayed so strong. *Lost so much.*

Tears burst through and rolled down her cheeks. She sobbed uncontrollably, letting go of everything she'd held inside for years. The harrowing injustice she'd fought against, the hope for the future of Tabiq she'd held in her heart. When he pulled her into his chest, her arms reached up and clung to him. *I don't want this jerk to hold me, but it's been so long since I've been held. So long since my father's arms held me and soothed me. I've been so alone.*

"Let it all out, Ziva."

She didn't want to enjoy being held by him. How was it possible his strength was becoming hers? This was a man she wanted to hate. He was evil, yet here she was drawn to him. *What kind of person am I? Am I just as bad as he is? I know what he's done, but I couldn't pull the trigger. I couldn't stop him. Whatever he does now is my fault. I'm as guilty as he is.*

Even with that knowledge, she couldn't pull away. Alex wiped the tears from her cheeks. She raised her head to look at him, another mistake. His eyes were as soft as she'd dreamed they'd be. As his head came toward hers, she closed her eyes and parted her lips in anticipation.

He didn't claim her lips roughly, as she thought he would. Instead, he was so gentle and tender that she quivered from the touch. Ziva wanted to pull him closer. She wanted to hide in the feeling of calm and forget the emotional turmoil she always felt.

"Ziva." His voice was husky against her lips.

Her name never sounded so sweet. She wanted to hear him call her name again and again. Ziva's hand ran down his bare chest, and Alex covered hers with his. His tongue traced her lips before darting inside. He tasted like sugar and coffee as her tongue entwined with his.

She needed more, so much more. "Alex I . . . I."

Then she pulled herself away. This may be what she wanted, but it wasn't right. He was Alex Henderson, the man who just forced himself on a poor girl. No matter what she thought she wanted, it wasn't this. *It couldn't be this.*

Pushing herself away from him, she ran back into her room and out the door, slamming it behind her. She needed to get away from him. Not for his sake but for hers. She thought she had the strength and fortitude to finish what she'd started. She was wrong. He was a charmer. A snake and master manipulator. *He'd have me in his bed, thinking he could control me too. It won't happen. Not now, not ever.*

Chapter Seven

Alex was left standing alone, wrapped in a towel, with his entire body throbbing. It wasn't how he pictured it to end when he kissed Ziva. Then again, he hadn't anticipated her pulling a gun on him either. *She has me tied up in knots, but damn, tied up by her is pretty damn sweet.*

Even if he was dressed, Alex wouldn't have followed after her. Ziva might not know it, but that was exactly what he needed her to do. Walking to his bed, Alex picked up his SAT phone and called Bennett.

"She's just about to leave the hotel."

"Got it."

"Whatever you do, don't let her see you." Alex had no idea why he was wasting his breath. Bennett was damn good at what he did, and Ziva was so flustered she wasn't going to be paying attention to her surroundings. Things couldn't have worked out more perfectly.

Unless Ziva and I were in a different place and time. Because I wouldn't have let her go, and she would've never left.

"Don't worry. I'll be able to track her truck from this shithole of a room if I have to. Is there anything I should know?"

"She was armed." Alex wasn't sure if she had more than the one gun, but Bennett needed to know. "She pulled a gun on me."

"Fuck! I never saw that coming."

"Neither did I," Alex admitted. She was a lot of things, but violent wasn't one of them. Since she didn't pull the trigger, he was betting he was right.

"This changes things. We need to—"

"It changes nothing. She was only out to protect Myla. Nothing more."

"Alex. You don't know what she's capable of," Bennett warned.

"You're right. But I'm telling you, Bennett, nothing better happen to her. If she pulls another gun, you better fucking find a way to disarm her without injuring her. If anything happens to her, you're answering to me. Got it?"

There was a brief pause but Bennett agreed. "We're playing a dangerous game, Alex. We still have no idea who she's working with. This could be a trap."

"Then I suggest you keep your eyes open. In the meantime, I'm going to pay the manager a visit. It's time we discuss his boss."

"I can't be there to back you up if I'm following Ziva."

"I'm not asking you to."

"Alex, I think you're in over your head. Hell, we both are. Look around. This place is so damn toxic; I'm not sure you can save it."

Bennett was right. Saving Tabiq was going to take a hell of a lot more than their efforts alone. That didn't mean he couldn't put a dent into the smooth-running corrupt machine. *I am going to shut this hotel down. I'm going to find my mother, and I will make sure nothing happens to Ziva if it's the last thing I do.*

"It's not all bad, Bennett. Look at Ziva. If she hasn't shown you the decent side of Tabiq, you're blind."

"Then get her to leave this place. I'm telling you, there is no way you can accomplish what you want to do all by yourself."

"Funny, I thought I had you covering my six." Alex tried to make light of the subject.

"You Hendersons are always looking for a miracle."

"Nothing wrong with expecting significant results. Now go and get me some."

"Roger."

Alex disconnected the call and headed back to the bed where he'd tossed her gun. Picking it up, he realized it weighed less than it should. Sliding an eject button, he pulled out the clip. It was empty. *She's crazy. Pulling a gun on someone is one thing. My guess is she probably wouldn't have pulled the trigger. But not to have it loaded . . . If I were anyone else, this would've ended so differently. And she wouldn't have been able to run away. And yet, seeing her with the gun in her hand had been sexy as hell. She's gorgeous. And to taste her lips . . .*

It only solidified his initial thought. They had to find Ziva. She was going to get herself killed if they didn't. If he thought they were playing a dangerous game, it was nothing compared to what she was doing. *I'll find you.* There wasn't anyone else who'd protect her. All she had was him, and she didn't even know they were on the same side.

Do nothing while waiting for Bennett to report back wasn't Alex's style. He needed to stay busy. Walking to his suitcase, he grabbed some clean clothes. He needed to reach out to the manager. Now seemed like a good time. He wasn't exactly sure what he was going to say to convince him to introduce him to his boss. *Not sure playing it by ear is the way to go on this, but I need to get a feel of the situation first.*

Alex could almost hear Bennett complaining. No one agreed with how Alex handled things. *Good thing I don't report to any of them.*

While he was dressing, his phone rang. It should've been Bennett, but to his surprise it was Brice. He didn't recall providing him with the secure line. That meant Bennett and Brice had been chatting. *Thanks for the heads-up, Bennett. I owe you one.*

"What is it, Brice?"

"What's the status?" Brice asked.

"Sun is shining. The water is great."

"Cut the shit, Alex. I know you're in Tabiq. I know you're looking for your mother. You should've waited for me."

"Brice, you had no intention of ever telling me what was going on. It's obvious Bennett reports to you, but don't forget . . . I don't," Alex barked at his brother.

"You have the right to know what we do. I know how you operate. You're hot-headed and stubborn. Two things that will get you killed over there. You don't know who you're dealing with."

"No, I don't, so why don't you tell me?" It was better late than never. Of course, he wasn't sure Brice actually had any valuable information. If he had, Bennett would've told him by now. *Or not. My character judgment is lacking lately.*

"The corruption goes right to the top. We cannot go in and take down the local level. If we do, it will reappear with different people in charge. We have to start at the top."

"That's what I'm trying to do. I was going to meet with the manager to set up a meeting."

"You're one Henderson. Think about it, Alex. What do you think they'll do if there was two or even three?"

"What are you talking about?"

"I'm on my way, and I'm not alone."

Fuck. This news is the last thing I wanted or needed. "You might as well turn around. I don't need you."

"Alex, that's where you're wrong. You need us, no different than we need you."

It was the first time Brice had ever spoken to him in such a manner. Actually, Brice wasn't a big talker.

Something must be up to have him opening up like this. *And it's not just being married.* "I'm not alone, Brice. But then again, I'm sure you already knew that."

"I did."

"Then you know why I'm here, and what I'm doing."

"And I know it's a dangerous game to play. They might think you're like our father now, but eventually, your true colors will come through, and then you're fucked."

"I'm a better actor than you might think." *God knows I've been lying and hiding things from you all my life. I'm sure I can pull a scam on one guy. No issue. No worry.*

"Alex, wake the hell up. We want to help. You're not the only one who has a mother there. Or have you forgotten that part?"

"No, I haven't."

"Good, then get ready because our plane touches down in four hours. Do not meet with the manager or anyone else until we talk face to face."

"And you don't think they're going to question why we're all coming to town now, out of the blue?" Alex didn't think Brice thought this through at all. *All my hard work will go up in smoke, once they figure out it's all a lie.*

"It's not all of us. Dean and I are coming. And no, they won't question anything except the color of our money."

Alex saw the greed here firsthand. But were they really going to be that naïve? He wasn't so sure.

"Alex, you're the one who doesn't plan and jumps in with both feet and your eyes closed. What's changed?"

It was a good question. *Maybe I'm not only thinking about myself.* "That's a question I should be asking you. I know how you like every detail set in stone."

"That I do. I had only two choices: do it my way and watch you get yourself killed or join this fucking crazy idea of yours."

Their family had never told each other how they felt. This conversation and group effort was the closest any of them came to expressing sibling love. It was unfamiliar, and yet Alex found it comforting. He'd been willing to do this alone. Hell, he knew the consequences and prepared himself for the worst. Having Brice and Dean here would be great moral support, but he didn't know how they were going to help if a shootout took place. *I don't want them in danger. They have their wives, but I have no one, so it doesn't matter if I go down.*

"Are just you and Dean on the jet?"

Brice laughed. "On the jet, yes. There is a commercial flight that should arrive shortly before we do. I believe Bennett has a few friends coming to the party."

"A few?"

"I don't ask questions. Sometimes it's better I don't know."

Alex laughed. *I don't think he'd tell us if we asked.* "Must be jet lag, because you don't sound like the brother I grew up with."

"Having a family of my own has changed my perspective. Lena's shown me what *normal* is supposed to be. Who knows, maybe after you get the answers you've been searching for, you'll think about settling down?"

It was something Alex had contemplated over the years, but he'd never found anyone he pictured spending the rest of his life with. It would take a special woman. One who understood he hated being tied down. *Even someone as intriguing as Ziva would tire of me.*

His brothers might be able to handle being stuck behind a desk and running business meetings. That wasn't him. Even when they were young, and their father made them all work at Poly-Shyn in the family business, he intentionally screwed up so his father would kick him out.

That's why he enjoyed his career as a novelist. He was free to travel any place anytime, and live the adventures he wrote about. Settling down would eliminate that.

"I think the single life is for me."

"I remember saying those exact words. Now I can't picture my life without Lena. And being a father, damn, it's a good feeling."

He was glad Brice enjoyed his life. But it wasn't for him, and telling him that would be like talking to a wall. *Never listened to anyone before. I don't think you've changed that much.*

"If you're done with my love life advice, how about sharing your brilliant idea on how we meet the big guys?"

"We ask for more. More than the local guy can provide. Tell them we're willing to pay, but we want to see the ladies first. And that we're not thrilled with the arrangements at the hotel. Our father may've been willing to stay in something substandard, but we're not."

"Yeah, that'll piss the manager off. And what exactly do you think that'll do?"

"He'll go running to his boss, who will want to keep us happy at all costs. Our name has a reputation here, Alex. I say let's use it to our benefit."

"I like the way you're thinking. Let's show these assholes that dear ole Dad wasn't as tough as his sons are," Alex added. He figured the people here would eat up that lie in a blink of an eye.

"See you when we land. Can you update Bennett with the change of plans?"

"Will do." Alex would call Bennett, but right now he needed Bennett to stay on the current assignment. *Follow Ziva and make sure nothing happens to her.*

It all sounded good in theory, but there was one thing Alex hadn't mentioned. *Finding and protecting Ziva.*

ZIVA DROVE DOWN the winding road, rip-roaring mad at Alex. He was so damn arrogant to think he was above the law. *If we had any laws that prevented such things.* He'd brushed everything off, as though he hadn't hurt Myla at all. As though Myla hadn't been in his room, in his bed. His actions were despicable.

And even though he knows I know everything he did, he still had the audacity to kiss me. Ziva brought her right hand up and slammed it into the steering wheel in frustration. She was angry at Alex and had every right to be. But she'd kissed him back. *Hell, I practically gave him an invitation. What kind of woman am I? How can I think of anything other than disdain for him?*

Ziva pulled up and parked the truck behind the trees as she had earlier with Myla. This time she stomped her way to the cabin. Each time her foot made contact with the ground, she pictured it crushing Alex's foot.

It was funny, because the worst thing she could think about doing was stomping on his toes, yet she'd pulled a gun on him. What had she been thinking? A man like that wasn't afraid of someone like her. It'd been written all over his face as she'd ordered him around. Alex had played along, only until he had the upper hand. *Which wasn't too long.* Ziva could pretend to be fierce, but he obviously knew she'd never pull the trigger. *And it wouldn't have done any good since it wasn't loaded.*

She pictured Alex laughing when he picked up the gun and saw it had no bullets. He didn't take her seriously before, and this wouldn't resolve that issue.

Myla ran out of the cabin to greet her. That wasn't supposed to be; they were supposed to be more careful than that. Then again, she wasn't sure she'd taken the time to explain all the ins and outs to Myla. She'd been so focused on seeing Alex and making him pay she hadn't paid attention to what was important. *These girls.*

"Myla. You need to wait in the cabin and be very quiet until I give the signal that it's safe to come out. What would've happened if Mr. Henderson had been with me?"

"Why should I be afraid of him?" Myla asked.

Ziva felt bad for Myla. She didn't comprehend that being sexually assaulted was wrong. *Maybe she's in shock. Or just in denial. Whatever it is, I can't push or she might have a breakdown. She'll figure it out on her own.*

"He isn't a very nice man."

"Why don't you like him, Ziva?" Myla asked sincerely.

She had to reply with something. *But what? Everything I say could be an emotional trigger for her.* Ziva decided to use herself as an example. "He kissed me."

The words were simple and far from being too much. Actually, that was all Alex had done to her. *It isn't technically a lie.*

Myla smiled. "Did you like it?"

Ziva was shocked. That wasn't the response she was expecting. "Myla, he should not kiss me after kissing you. That's wrong." She hoped that would make it clearer to her.

Myla shook her head. "He did not kiss me."

"Of course, he kissed you."

"No, he didn't."

Ziva reached her hand out and touched Myla's arm. Speaking very gently, she said, "Myla, you don't have to lie. It's okay. I know what happens when the manager takes girls to a man."

"I do too, but Mr. Henderson didn't do that. He said . . ." Myla looked down, "I can't tell you. I'm sorry. I promised."

"Promised who?"

"Mr. Henderson. I promised never to tell anyone."

She had to find out what the secret was. If it had to do with Alex, it couldn't be good. Ziva hated using manipulation, but she was desperate.

"Myla. I told you he kissed me. Would he kiss me if he didn't trust me?" Myla shook her head. "Then he would say it's okay for you to tell me. Maybe I can help."

"I don't want him to be angry with me. Not after what he said he'd do to help my family."

"Help them?" Ziva remembered her saying something about her family yesterday, but she assumed it was a threat to harm them. "What is he going to do?"

"Give them money so they can go someplace where my baby sisters won't be sold. He's going to send Mama and Papa so we can all be together. After this is all done, he said I could go too. Can you imagine, Ziva, a place where you can play outside, and not worry about the police coming for you?"

It was a dream she had every night. One she wished she could deliver. She was only able to help a few at a time. Was it possible Alex honestly was going to help Myla and her family? If so, why?

"Did he say why?"

"No. Mr. Henderson only said he needed my help."

It was all coming down to this one question. The one that would say what kind of man Alex Henderson truly was. "What did he need you to do?"

Myla blushed. "He said I must pretend that I had serviced him if anyone asked. And I couldn't tell anyone the truth because if I did, they'd know he was lying too."

"He never touched you? Not at all?"

"No. He slept on the couch and gave me the bed. He was very kind to me."

Ziva believed Myla was telling her the truth. There was no reason for her to lie. *At least, not at this time.* She didn't understand why Alex paid for a virgin at the hotel and then hadn't touched her. *Was it some game to him? Was Alex testing the waters for next time? Or maybe what I said to him when I took him to see the prison opened his eyes.*

"Did he ever say why he was here if not to have . . . you?"

Myla nodded. "He is looking for his mother."

"Mother? Here?"

"Yes. He knows his mother was ripped from her family and sold to his father. He wants to find her and punish the people who are doing this to us. So now you know why I'm not afraid of him."

That I do. Why didn't he tell me? Why let me believe he was like his father? She knew the answer. *Because he doesn't trust me.*

It hurt her, and she didn't know why. The important thing was he was here, trying to do good. Although his heart was in the right place, Ziva knew it'd take more than one man to take the corruption down. After all, this had been going on in Tabiq for more than forty years. His mother might be dead by now . . . *How did he expect to find her?*

Then she thought back to the bag of weapons. If he was such a good man, why bring an arsenal and hide it in the closet? If he had given them to the manager in exchange for Myla, that might make sense, but the manager would've demanded payment before Alex stepped foot in the hotel. It was a smooth-running operation. *It might be smooth, but it's immoral as heck.*

She had some of the answers, but she still had a boatload of questions. Of course, after she aimed a gun at his chest, he probably didn't want to see her again. *Then again, he kissed me after that. Maybe he's not as angry as I thought he was. I've been wrong about so much regarding him. I don't like it, but I'm glad I was wrong.*

"Thank you for telling me, Myla. I can help him now."

Myla beamed a big beautiful smile. "Just like you're helping the other girls and me."

"Something like that." Ziva smiled and walked to the cabin.

Since she was here, she might as well make herself useful and cook dinner for them. Ziva was used to eating alone. Actually, everything she did was by herself. Until she met Alex, she never thought twice about it being different. Yet, since she took him on their little excursion, she yearned for something more. Even though their conversation had been harsh, it had been nice to be listened to as an equal. When she thought back to that day, armed with the knowledge from Myla, she saw a very different Alex Henderson in her mind. He had listened to her and still challenged her. Unlike any man before, he truly seemed interested in what she'd told him. The men of Tabiq barely registered the opinion of a female, let alone took the time to hear what was being said. She knew American men were different, but compared to his peers, Alex still stood out. Not once had he been condescending. It was refreshing to have a voice. *If only it was for more than a brief moment in time and for more than just me. All women should feel as I had. An opportunity to be our own advocate about how we want to live our lives.*

Ziva was content doing what she was doing. *But it'd be nice to have someone by my side. Someone who'd hold me and understand if I cry when I am too late to save one of the girls.*

That was asking a lot of a person. The mission with these girls was the commitment she'd made. It wasn't something she could ask another person to join her on. It wasn't only hard work; it was risking your life, knowing at any time someone could see her and turn her in to the police. There would be no trial to determine guilt or innocence. No one would visit her in jail. She'd be taken away and never seen again.

Why would I ever ask someone I love to do the same? If I

love them, the last thing I'd want is for them to be in harm's way.

Ziva wasn't saying that she loved Alex, but she was fond of him. The more she learned about him, the more she liked him. He'd kept things from her, and she'd done the same. Her reason was she didn't trust him based on who his father was. That was wrong. Of course, he purposely let her believe the worst about him. It was odd, and she didn't understand.

Myla set the table with the other girls, while Ziva brought the rice and beans from the stove. The table was set when one of the girls who'd been on lookout rushed inside.

"Ziva, I saw a man in the trees. He is coming this way," the girl exclaimed breathlessly.

Ziva quickly dropped the pan on the table and rushed to the door. She peered outside but saw no one. She turned to the girls and said, "I want you all to stay inside. Don't come out unless I call for you. Do you understand?"

They nodded. Then she turned to Myla. "If I don't come back, I need you to take my car and find Mr. Henderson. Bring him here and tell him everything. Understand?"

"You should not go out there, Ziva."

"I have to, Myla. I need to get him away from here."

Ziva handed the keys to her truck to Myla and left the cabin. She quickly made her way through the woods. She could see the man off in the distance. He was heading toward the cabin. How had he found them? Who was he? She needed to think fast.

Looking around, she found a branch on the ground, brought it to her knees, and cracked it. It made a loud snapping sound that echoed. She looked up, and the man saw her. She began to run through the trees away from the cabin. He chased her. Every step she took bought the girls more time to hide. She'd taught them well, now she hoped they'd listened to everything she'd said.

Ziva heard the man getting closer. Her heart was pounding hard in her chest as she maneuvered through the trees, ducking under the low branches and leaping over fallen limbs. *Don't give up, Ziva. Just a bit farther and you'll be at the river. If he can't swim, you may have a chance to get away.*

She could hear the sounds of the rushing water echoing in the wind. She was so close, *only a few more yards.*

It was over in a heartbeat. In front of her stood a second man. *There were two of them?* He had his gun drawn and aimed at her. She came to an abrupt stop and collapsed onto her knees.

"Ms. Gryzb, what are you doing out here so far from the station?" one of the police officers asked.

"Maybe she wanted to pick berries," the one from behind said sarcastically.

The two men laughed. Ziva knew it was over. They knew who she was, and no matter what she said, the way they were looking at her told her everything. She'd been so distracted after leaving Alex she missed them tailing her. It was a high-price mistake. *My life. The girls . . .*

Ziva had so many regrets. *Not able to finish what I started. Not telling Alex I'm sorry for judging so wrongly.*

For leaving his room when I so badly wanted to stay in his arms.

She sensed the men only inches away from her now. Closing her eyes, she waited for what was about to come. Instead, she felt a sharp pain in the back of her head, then all went black.

Chapter Eight

"SORRY MR. HENDERSON, but we caught this... girl, trying to get away. If she doesn't please you, we can send another at no charge."

Alex glared at the manager. He was shaking on the inside, trying damn hard to control himself. The only thing holding him back was his concern about why Myla was here. He knew she was with Ziva. Bennett had already called and confirmed their location. *So, what made you risk your life to come back here?*

So not to want any further question, Alex grabbed Myla by the bicep a bit roughly and tugged her into the room. "I like this one just fine." Then he slammed the door in the manager's face.

Once Alex heard his footsteps leaving, he turned to Myla and asked, "What happened? Why are you here?"

Myla looked at where Alex still held her.

He released her right away. "I'm sorry. I didn't mean to hurt you. I needed him to think I was not happy with you."

"I know. It's okay. Don't worry about me. We need

to help Ziva."

His heart sank. "Is she hurt?"

"Men came and took her away. She wasn't moving. I'm afraid of what they're going to do to her."

Alex was beside himself. He should've been there instead of waiting for Brice and Dean to show up. From what Bennett had told him, the place seemed secure. Either he was wrong, or something had changed.

"Do you know who they were?"

Myla nodded. "They are the police. Or at least, that's what they call themselves. We have no real police here. They all work for . . . well we don't really know who they work for, but they are not here to protect the people. They do whatever they are told, and it usually isn't good, at least not for us. I saw the men who came to the cabin and took Ziva talking to the hotel manager before. They are very dangerous men, and they hurt Ziva."

"How do you know she was hurt?" *Please don't let it be bad.*

"I was hiding, but I saw one of them hit her in the head. She wasn't moving when they carried her away. I hope she isn't—"

"I'm sure she's not." *God, she better not be.* He needed to find her, but he had no clue where to start looking. Pounding the manager's face until he divulged the information sounded like a place to start. If he went in empty-handed, he wasn't going to be alive long enough to ask any questions and positively not long enough to beat the shit out of the guy.

Alex grabbed his SAT phone and called Bennett. He quickly brought him up to date with the details Myla had just told him.

"That road isn't heavily traveled. Those goons had to have been waiting and watching her already. I was afraid something was going to happen. The Turchettas aren't here but have been observing the cabin via satellite. I'll see if they have a location or some footage for us."

"If you knew she was in danger, why the fuck did you leave?" Alex barked over the phone.

"I figured she was safe until you made your move. That's when I expected things to go to hell. If they were watching her, it's because she's doing something outside of being associated with you. We need to find out what that is."

Alex looked at Myla and asked, "Do you trust me?"

She nodded.

"Then I need you to tell me what Ziva was doing in those woods. I need to know everything you can think of. It might be our only way to find her." He looked her square in the eyes, practically pleading for her cooperation. Ziva's life depended on what Myla could tell them.

"She finds girls who are young but will soon be of age to be . . . taken. She hides them away and takes care of them so the manager's men can't find them. She brings them food, clothes, books, and everything else they need. They all know they can't leave the area because someone might see them. No one would break the rule. Each girl knows the price if they are discovered."

"Did they find you? I mean all of the girls?"

"No. We take turns as lookout. When the men were spotted, Ziva left the cabin and led them away from us. She told me if she didn't come back, to take her truck and come find you and to tell you everything. She will need you to protect the girls, as you protected me."

Ziva was even braver than he imagined. Not only had she confronted him, but she took on armed men to save the lives of others. *Don't be dead, Ziva. I'm coming for you. I'll find you. You just have to believe and trust.*

"How do you know this if she told you to stay put?"

"I couldn't let her go by herself. But when I saw the man hit her on the head and put her on his shoulder, I knew there wasn't anything to do except get you."

"You are very brave, Myla."

Alex lifted the phone back to his ear. "Did you get all that?"

"I did. It doesn't look good, Alex."

He didn't need Bennett to tell him what he already knew. "I say we go directly to the manager, and demand he brings her to us."

"He'll deny they have her. Hell, he'll pretend he doesn't know who she is."

Alex needed something that would make him cough her up. Then he remembered what Brice said. *"They only care about the color of your money."*

"Bennett, I'm going to talk to the manager. I'm going to request he locates the woman who was in the room next door. I'll offer him a shitload of money if I can have her for the night. If he's as greedy as we think he is, he'll release her to me."

"That's a consequential risk, Alex. He might put two and two together, and you'll disappear right along with Ziva."

"Then I guess we're about to see how good of a shot you are. Because I'm going down."

"You should wait for Brice and Dean."

"I need you to have the men you have stashed around get Myla and the other girls to safely. Explain to Brice exactly what you heard, and get them the hell out of harm's way."

"I'm not leaving you to enter this alone."

"I won't be. I'll be with Ziva." Alex disconnected the call and turned back to Myla. "A man named Bennett is going to take you to my brothers. They will not hurt you. I need you to make sure the other girls know they can trust them too, okay?"

Myla nodded. "Are you truly going to go save Ziva?"

The look in Myla's eyes said she knew the score. It wasn't hopeful. That didn't mean he wasn't going to move forward with his plan. He was her best hope right now. *If anything happens to her, I don't know what I'll do.* Alex was as ready as he could be. Like Myla, he knew the risk. "I'm going to try."

Alex left Myla alone in the room while he went downstairs. He'd slammed the door in the manager's face, so he wasn't so sure how happy he'd be to see him again. When he arrived in the lobby, the manager met him with a grin. *Oh, that's right. You don't care how I treat you as long as I pay you.*

"Mr. Henderson. Is there something you require?"

"Let's talk in private," Alex stated.

With a nod, the manager led him to a back room. Once the door was closed, he asked, "What do you require that needs such privacy?"

"There was a woman I had arranged to use the adjoining room. I can't find her. I want her." With a sick growl, he said, "I need her."

"I'm sorry. I don't believe she's staying at this hotel any longer."

"You don't understand. I'll pay anything to have her one more night." Alex watched his eyes widen. *Yes. Take the bait and give me Ziva. Hell, I will pay whatever you ask as long as you don't harm her.*

Nothing was more important than her safety. Alex hadn't realized how much he'd come to care for her until now. He couldn't let anyone else see that, or it would ruin the entire plan. They needed to think this was a business transaction for services.

"You are not pleased with the other girl?"

"I am. I want both."

The manager grinned. "I understand such needs. Unfortunately, the young woman you speak about is no longer able to come to this hotel."

"Why is that?" *Don't you dare tell me she's dead.*

"Other accommodations have been made for her."

"Then unmake them. I. *Want.* Her."

The manager peered at Alex for a long time. "I believe arrangements can be made. You'd need to leave immediately to join her. One million US dollars, then you may join her for one night."

Join her? His back was up against the wall. He either agreed now and left to go to God knows what location, or he might never see Ziva again. Alex had to go with his gut, and hope the Turchettas had been able to get something on the satellite imaging. Otherwise, Bennett wouldn't be able to find him, any more than he could find Ziva.

"Five nights, two million dollars. That is my only offer." The truth was he'd pay whatever they asked, as long as Ziva was unharmed. They already held too many cards and he wasn't about to reveal his hand. Not this deep in the game. He needed to buy as much time as he could. Changing their offer was the only thing he could think of. *If Bennett can't pull it off and find us, then as least Ziva and I will have five nights together.* He knew he was playing a dangerous game. There was no doubt in Alex's mind that if any of these guys felt they were being set up, he and Ziva would most likely be killed.

He'd put himself in compromising situations many time before for research on his books, but this had nothing to do with anything other than finding her. *I'll find her, even if it means losing myself.*

The manager peered at him and Alex feared he'd pushed too far. If he had any hope of seeing Ziva again, he needed this work. *Let his greed blind him.*

The manager said sharply, "Agreed."

It was done. He hoped this wasn't a mistake. If he had any chance of saving Ziva, seeing her again, he'd take it.

"Then come with me and transfer the money. Once it's received, we leave."

Alex knew it would only take minutes for the wire to go through. It was all in Bennett's hands now.

HER HEAD WAS killing her. That was a good sign. It meant she was still alive. For how long had yet to be determined. It was dark, but by the bouncing around and the smell of exhaust, Ziva knew she was being transported in a trunk of a car.

She listened intently. They must be in a town because she could hear voices when they stopped and horns beeping along the way. If she knew how long she'd been knocked out, maybe she could estimate her location. Ziva had no idea if it had been minutes or hours. *Maybe days by how stiff I am.*

Ziva felt around for the emergency release lever. When she found it, she contemplated pulling it or waiting. It wasn't like anyone was going to come to her rescue if they saw her leaping from a moving police car. If anything, they'd shout out and let them know she was trying to escape. It wasn't that they didn't want to help her, they didn't want to pay the price for aiding and abetting.

She knew there wasn't a way out for her. They might keep her alive long enough to see what information they could get out of her, but when her usefulness ran out, so would her time. *Might as well just kill me now, because I'm not going to tell you where the girls are or how many I have. And I most definitely am not going to tell you about Alex's plan.*

Knowing he'd come here to help put a stop to all this madness was comforting. She'd have been happier if he'd told her himself. All the misunderstanding between them had wasted time they couldn't get back. Instead of plotting the different ways she'd make him suffer for his actions, she could've thought of the different positions she'd try with him. She'd had a lover before. It wasn't anything that had her blood roaring. Yet there was something different about Alex. Maybe it was the forbidden fruit. Whatever it was he could make her melt, and she loved and hated it at the same time.

Ziva wasn't innocent, but it'd been a long time since she'd had a lover. If his kiss was any indication what it would've been like to be in his arms, she knew it would've been explosive. His gentle kiss had her body tingling all over. At the time she hated him and herself for it. Now she longed to taste his lips one more time.

If only I could see him once more; there's so much I'd say. Ziva made a mental note of where she'd start. There was so much to say, yet nothing came to mind. She would walk up to him, wrap her arms around him, and hold him tight as though she'd never let go. She wasn't sure someone like Alex Henderson, so good-looking and strong, would want to be with her.

Funny how all I want is something simple. Yet, right now it would be the best thing in the world. For all the things I have to say, saying nothing is best.

The vehicle came to an abrupt stop, and she heard the doors open and close. She'd arrived; she just wished she knew where.

"We have come all this way. Why turn back now?" one man asked.

"Not our job to question. The less we know, the better. When we get there, we turn her over to him. If he wants her dead, then let him dig the damn hole himself."

They both laughed. "He can throw them both in for all I care. We get paid the same either way."

Both? Oh, God. No. Please don't tell me they have Myla too. She'd told her to go for help. Leaving the cabin was so risky. Had they snatched her along the way?

"What I don't understand is why there? We were told to make her disappear and then told to take her to the finest home in Tabiq. The manager must be drunk on wine again."

"He offered to pay us each fifty US dollars extra to get her there unharmed."

"Shit. He should've told us that before I hit her over the head with the butt of the gun. Do you think they will notice?"

"We will say we found her that way. If she says otherwise, we hit her again." The first man laughed wickedly.

Ziva was more puzzled now than before. She'd known her fate. She was being sent someplace unexpected now. *They really must think I know more than I do. Wait till they find out it's all a waste of time.*

She heard the key in the lock and the trunk burst open. The bright sunshine caused her to squint and turn her face away. One of the men reached in and roughly picked her up.

"Easy. Remember, no marks or no extra money."

The guy loosened his hold. "Oh, yeah. Too bad. I was going to have fun with this one. She's feisty."

Oh yes, I am. And trust me, I wouldn't be the only one with marks on me when you were done. "Where are you taking me?"

"The boss said someone requested your company, and we have to deliver you."

Who the heck would want me? Twenty-nine is not considered young, and I'm no virgin. I must be on the bargain shopper's list. It was sick that she joked in her own mind about such things. Was she so desensitized she no longer valued her own existence? She should be scared of dying, but her body ached too much to trouble her. Ziva never expected to live as long as she had. Each day, she had wondered if it were her last. She always feared someone knew what she'd been up to and would turn her in. The day had arrived. She had regrets, but not the ones she thought she would. Ziva had done the best she could. Although she was disappointed at how few she'd helped, she was surprised she'd been able to help any at all.

The men placed a blindfold over her eyes and had her sit in the backseat of the car. "Get down. We don't want anyone to see you. It's going to be a long ride and a long night for you from what we hear. You might as well get your sleep." The man laughed again.

Fighting his instructions would only cause more pain. She complied with one request, but she wasn't about to sleep. Although she tried to fight it, the pounding in her head continued, and darkness once again overtook her.

Chapter Nine

I AGREED TO this, but I sure as hell wish I knew where they're taking me. Not that I have any way to let Bennett or anyone else know what the fuck is going on. All Alex could do was hope Bennett had been close by and watched when they left the hotel. Without his SAT phone or regular cell phone, there would be no way to communicate except through the goons driving.

If he did have his phone, he'd tell Bennett to stay on task, keep Myla safe. The goal had changed since they last spoke. He needed to locate Ziva. If what the manager told him was true, he was on his way to meet her. That seemed far-fetched because for the last eight hours he'd been riding around in the back of a black Lincoln Town Car. The island wasn't big enough to take that long to go from one end to the other. They were stalling for some reason. He'd played their game long enough. If they kept driving for much longer, it would become nightfall, and he wanted to arrive in the light of day to have a clue as to where he was.

Alex was pretty good with tracking his bearings.

These guys were intentionally stalling. There were only a few reasons why they'd delay like that. *Either they don't have Ziva, or something's happened to her, and they're trying to find a suitable substitute. Good luck. She's . . . like no one I've ever met before.*

She's . . . important to me.

There was something so unique about her. Ever since she stumbled into him several days before, he hadn't been able to get her out of his mind. He'd wanted to pull her into his arms and kiss her then and there. Yet, he hadn't allowed himself to be distracted by her loveliness. And a distraction was exactly what she turned out to be.

Even now, when he was supposed to be meeting Brice and Dean, Alex couldn't focus on anything but Ziva. For all he cared, his brothers could board their jet and head back to the States. He wasn't going anywhere until he had Ziva safe with him. *If anything's happened to her, I'm not returning. I'm going down, taking out as many of these bastards as I can.*

"You do know where we're going, right?" Alex asked as they passed the same building for the third time.

"We're waiting on instructions."

"Here's one. Stop this fucking car and let me out. I'm a busy man and don't have time for your boss's games," Alex said. He needed to get to where they were holding Ziva. His gut told him she was alive and close by.

"It won't be much longer."

"Pull over now!" Alex needed these guys nervous

about him changing his mind. That a major deal was falling through. If he was correct, they'd panic and call the boss for direction.

Sure enough, one guy pulled out his phone. He rattled off in Tabiqian. Alex didn't need to know what was said. The guy's body language said he'd just got his ass chewed out.

"You will be at your destination in a few minutes."

Gee, we're that close? How surprising is that? Alex shot the guy a look that probably matched what his boss had just said. He mumbled something under his breath in Tabiqian again as they turned away from the city.

Making their way down a long winding road, they came to a house that didn't fit with what he'd seen so far on the island. There was a massive iron gate with two guards stationed at the entrance, dressed in black, and each armed with an M-16. The car slowly drove to the gate and stopped. The driver rolled down his dark tinted window and whispered something to the guard, who then peered into the backseat.

The guard glared at Alex as though trying to intimidate him. Alex wanted to meet his stare and tell him to fuck off but needed to remind himself he was playing a role here. One that required him to cave to the bastard. It wasn't easy, but he forced himself to look away first. *Enjoy it now. Next time we meet, I promise, I won't be looking away.*

Once the guard was satisfied Alex wasn't a threat, he straightened and waved the vehicle through. As they moved forward, the massive house became clearer. This wasn't just anyone's home. Was it possible he'd just found the location of the big boss? It was what he wanted, but now he was looking for something much more valuable to him. *Ziva.*

If this was the big boss's place, why would they have Ziva there? Alex knew what attracted her to him, but he knew they weren't looking at her for the same thing. He had a sinking feeling about this. If she was here, it wasn't to provide him with a good time. He actually hoped not to see Ziva.

Before they made it to the top of the hill, he saw a guard tower, much like the one at the prison. This one was staffed, and he sensed a gun trained on him. Alex started mentally preparing himself for a hostile welcome. *Maybe I wasn't so smooth with the manager after all. But he had no problem taking my money. That bastard will pay.*

They were still en route to the house when Alex looked down to the city below. If he hadn't known what Tabiq was all about, he would've thought it was a vacation place. The sight was spectacular. *Is this what you dream of when you think of home, Ziva? A place where families can raise their children, without living in fear from the government?* The hillside was covered with flowers in all directions, and the town was surrounded by lush green trees. *It's a wonderful dream, Ziva. Don't give it up. It's your home. Fight for what you want it to be.*

That seemed simple, coming from a man who lived in a country that had more comforts than anyone could ask for. But for Alex, he wasn't thinking about the places he lived, as much as he was the family he'd come from. Like the view below, it appeared to be ideal. It was the farthest thing from the truth. If it hadn't been for James Henderson having more money than God, he was sure the state would've knocked on their door and taken them away from their father. How any of his siblings survived the mental and physical abuse was beyond him. He thought about them and was amazed at what they had overcome. Alex, however, had never dealt with the grief and pain. Instead, he'd buried the pain in his stories. It made for great writing, but it left him one fucked-up individual. *Fucked-up just like Tabiq. I bet Ziva would look at me and see something redeemable, too. She'd be just as wrong as she is about Tabiq. Some things are too broken to be fixed. I'm one of them.*

He'd figured that out long ago. Everyone thought he was a deadbeat. They weren't far off, he was just dead on the inside. That's why he'd chosen the career he had. It gave him the escape from the truth he needed. If he hadn't, his family probably wouldn't speak to him. Instead, they all thought he was carefree, cracking a joke about everything. In reality, he struggled daily to find good in the god-awful world he'd had the misfortune to grow up in.

Looking once again to the city, he thought about Ziva. Here she was, a woman who had faced such adversity and hadn't hardened her heart. If anything, it molded her into the strong, loving, compassionate woman she was today. When Myla told him what Ziva had done, risking her life to protect those who had no one to fight for them, he wished he were half the human she was.

He was here to find his mother. Yes, he also wanted to crush the bastards. He'd even contemplated blowing this hellhole off the planet. But Ziva wasn't like that. She wasn't crushing the bad; she had searched for the good. And she was making a difference. *More than I will ever do. My quest is completely self-focused. Something I wanted to do for me. She is thinking of everyone but herself.*

He respected what she was trying to do, but he couldn't have her life in danger each day. If Myla hadn't come to him, Ziva would've been . . . killed. It was that simple. No one would ask any questions or care.

But I'm asking. I care. I need you to know that, Ziva. Someone cares very much. That was something he intended to make crystal clear when he set eyes upon her again.

The car finally stopped at the entrance of what he'd thought was just a home, but up close it was more like a fortress. There were iron bars on all the windows and doors. A burly man with evil in his eyes and a scar on his face came out the front door, carrying an M-16. This tense, heavily armed moment was not the welcoming committee one would expect after paying two million dollars for five nights with a woman. *Yeah. They know what I'm up to. Fuck! And they know I want Ziva.* He knew exactly why he was taken there. They were going to use Ziva to extort money from him. Alex wished it were as simple as they were planning on her sleeping with him. He knew that wasn't the case. That could've taken place at the hotel.

As he got out of the car and followed the guard inside, his fears were confirmed. Ziva was standing inside, hands behind her back, a blindfold over her eyes, and a gag in her mouth. Alex wanted to call out to her, let her know he was there and everything would be all right. His gut told him she didn't know who was there. *Sorry, but it's best to keep it that way for now.*

Another guard, this one taller than the first one, but just as evil looking, gave Ziva a hard nudge forward and asked, "Is this the woman you wanted?"

Alex flinched but uttered nothing, nodding his response.

"Take her away," the tall guard said as he once again pushed Ziva, this time away from Alex. Then he pointed to Alex and said, "The boss wants to see you."

Not as much as I want to see him. I wish I had a gun with me as my thank-you gift for having me. Bastard.

Two armed men approached from behind. Alex watched as they took Ziva away, dragging her by her arm. It was killing him to appear indifferent, witnessing her being mistreated. He knew it would be stupid to show any interest or fight them. Her only chance of getting out of this was if he could negotiate her release. *And maybe mine too.*

Once she was out of sight, the tall guard led him down a hallway and stopped in front of a large oak door. He knocked and then opened it. Alex couldn't wait to see the bastard's face. This sick piece of shit was one guy he wasn't going to turn away from. He was going to let him know exactly what he thought of him.

When he came around the corner and entered the room, he saw a large, dark cherry desk with intricately detailed carved birds on the legs. There was a large black leather wingback chair that faced away from them. Alex wanted to go over, spin it around, and knock the son of a bitch out.

"Boss, Henderson is here," the tall guard announced.

The chair slowly spun around. Alex almost dropped on the floor in disbelief. *There is no way. No fucking way.*

Alex had pictured the scum on so many different occasions, as big, tough, and ugly as hell. Everything that matched how he ruled this country. A cold-hearted, ruthless bastard. His mind was having a difficult time comprehending what he saw before him. *Impossible.*

He'd never imagined *the boss* was some high-class snooty woman, who appeared to be even tinier than Ziva and not much older. *There has to be some mistake. There is no way she is the one running this country. Who would fear her?*

Alex remembered his father hadn't looked particularly intimidating either. If you were to judge a book by its cover, James Henderson appeared to be wholesome. A father you'd see cheering on his son at a little league game. But his father never supported anything that any of his children had participated in. If anything, he'd tried to break what little self-confidence they had. He was a master manipulator and one of the cruelest men he'd ever had the displeasure of knowing.

But this? This woman? He was floored.

He could get past the boss wasn't what he expected, but he struggled to believe a woman would allow and dictate the selling and abuse of other females. He'd envisioned as a child that his life would've been so different had there been a woman in the house. Looking at the one sitting in front of him, he was no longer sure of that.

The look in her eyes contradicted her natural beauty. She was undoubtedly the one in control. *You'd have been the perfect match for my father.* "You're the boss?" Alex asked.

She removed her glasses and looked Alex over from head to toe. "You're not what I expected either." Her voice was a mixture of venomous and sultry.

I don't know why you brought me here, but it sure as hell isn't that. She was eyeing him as though he was dessert. *I'd take a bullet before I'd touch you, you sadistic bitch.*

Alex wasn't about to play whatever game she had in mind. He was here for one reason, and one reason only, and that was to take Ziva back with him. Once he'd seen her tied up, he knew it wasn't going to be as easy as he'd hoped. Now meeting the boss, it had gotten worse. For the first time, he was glad Bennett ignored his instructions and contacted Brice. If either he or Ziva had any hope of making it out alive, it was going to require some major help from the outside. He already knew there wasn't anyone in Tabiq who could be trusted. *The only one I trust is in the same boat as I am.*

"You know why I'm here," Alex said in a tone that said he wasn't amused at all.

"I do."

"Then let's cut the bullshit. Tell me what the price is." Alex knew it was all about money. Or so he thought.

"You insult my intelligence, Mr. Henderson. You come to my country and try to make a mockery out of me. If I let either of you go, the people will think I'm weak. My authority will no longer hold any power. No amount of money you offer is worth that."

He had to admit, she was feared throughout the country. He doubted many knew the boss was a woman.

"Then why am I here?" Alex wasn't sure he wanted to hear the answer, but it would determine his next move.

"Our families have a long history of working together. You come here so arrogantly, thinking you can change what was started by our fathers."

"What the fuck are you talking about?"

"I'm saying that Tabiq was a third-world country until your father came here. He was searching for a location to build a plant to support the growing plastic industry. He was told there was oil here, which he'd hoped would reduce the cost of production. When he discovered he was misled, and we had no oil to offer, he found another natural resource that was even more lucrative."

"Are you suggesting that my father encouraged Tabiq to partake in human trafficking?" Alex yelled from across the room.

She smiled at him. "Encouraged? I believe the word you're looking for is partnered."

Alex wanted to hurl. That was something he couldn't accept. This woman was telling him everything he'd ever known about his father, and their past, was a lie.

"My father was many things, including a shrewd businessman. There was no need to involve himself in such a disgusting enterprise."

"You believe because your father was so wealthy, he wasn't driven by wanting more? If that's what you believe, you know nothing about him. All he thought about was money and how to make more. I was told when my father presented his idea to James, your father leaped at the chance to invest with the others."

Others? Alex was gaining a lot of information. Unfortunately, he was sure she was only sharing it with him because she planned to kill him.

"You seem to know a lot about my family, yet I don't even know your name."

"Rajani."

Alex had hoped to recognize the name. Tie it somehow to anyone his father had dealt with. He wished he'd chosen to work at Poly-Shyn so he'd be up to date with their counterparts. *Then again, if they were anything like Rajani and her family, I'm glad I stayed out.* "It's not a name I'm familiar with."

"It was my father's name. It means dark."

Appropriate. So was bitch. "Who are these others you mentioned?"

"Businessman like your father. Investors."

"And what exactly did these investors do?" *Besides sleep with young women.*

"They put Tabiq on the map. Money draws more money. They let their friends know about the special accommodations we were able to provide."

"By accommodations you mean innocent young women."

"Oh, you naïve fool. We provide more than that."

Alex arched a brow. He wasn't sure what more there could be. "And what is that exactly?"

"None of your concern. I didn't bring you here to keep you up to date on my business. You're here so you understand I will not tolerate your interference in any way."

"And how do you believe you can stop me?"

"My dear Alexander, you really don't know who you're dealing with, do you? My father, like yours, is no longer alive. I run everything now and have for several years. Your father came here shortly before he passed. He never believed any of you would come *here* in search of your mothers, but he had a plan in place should that happen. And here you are," she said snidely as she looked him over from head to toe. "I can't decide if you are incredibly stupid or if he was right to be so arrogant in his forward planning."

Our father didn't care if we were killed in a quest for truth? Was the man pure evil? It wasn't a real question. Pure didn't come close to James's level of evil.

Alex wasn't sure who he hated more at this moment: his father or Rajani. It was something he could dispute forever and still not decide. He had more important things on his agenda. "Do you know who my mother is?"

Rajani smiled. "I take it you don't."

She hadn't answered his question. He only believed half of what she told him. As Rajani appeared to be a few years younger than he was, she wouldn't have been born when his father first came to Tabiq and . . . taken his mother. Although James didn't want them to find their mothers, he also hadn't been one who went to another for help. *Not even a so-called partner. I'm not buying it. She's bluffing.* At least that was what his gut was telling him. Either way, his patience had reached its limit. Snapping back, he said, "Don't fucking trifle with me, Rajani. I'm not my father, but you'd be making a huge mistake if you underestimated me."

Rajani glared at him before she chuckled. "You hold no power here. Unless you missed the armed guards outside my door as well as those surrounding the entire estate."

He hadn't missed a thing. That didn't mean he was about to bow to her will. She may run her country, but she sure as hell didn't run him. *This Henderson is going to make you wish you never heard our name.*

Alex had so many questions but needed to put some time and space between the two of them. The longer he could drag it out, the more likely he'd still be alive when the cavalry showed up. There was one thing left unaddressed.

"Why bring Ziva here?"

"So you would come."

"She means nothing to me. Let her go."

Rajani laughed. "There is only one way either of you is leaving this place. If you do not cooperate with my demands, she'll be the first to exit." Rajani leaned her arms onto the desk and met Alex's gaze as she said, "In a box, in pieces, that is."

Alex knew she meant exactly what she was saying. "What do you want me to do?" He was willing to do just about anything if it meant saving Ziva.

Rajani sat back in her leather chair. "We'll discuss this tomorrow. For now, you can be with this woman who means nothing to you. Enjoy it, because if you don't comply with my request tomorrow, it's all the time you two will ever have."

The guards came, grabbed Alex by the arms, and dragged him out of the office. It was hard holding back, especially when he wanted to choke the life out of that evil sadistic bitch, but he knew he was joining Ziva. Thinking they may only have tonight wasn't comforting. Yet, he wasn't going to share any of what he'd learned with Ziva. He'd fill her with hope that they'd be out of there soon. *And hopefully not in a box.*

Chapter Ten

Ziva had been tossed onto the floor, her right cheek making contact on impact. She was still so sore. Everything ached from being bounced around in the trunk of the car. If she hadn't known any better, she would've thought they'd beaten her. *I'm sure that is yet to come.*

She listened intensely, trying to hear if anyone was in the room with her. The only thing she could hear was the ticking of a clock. *Hopefully not a bomb.*

Ziva tried to stand. She rolled over and was able to get onto her knees. Pain shot through her right knee. She recalled smashing it on a rock when she'd dropped to her knees in surrender. It was only one of the injuries she'd suffered. Thorns on bushes had battered her legs as she ran from the police. She'd been wearing shorts and a T-shirt at the time, which hadn't offered much protection. The smell of dried blood filled her nostrils, and she tried not to heave.

She tried to steady herself to stand, yet as she did, the pain in the back of her head returned. With the blindfold snugly in place and her hands tightly duct taped behind her, she couldn't get her bearings enough to stand. Giving up, Ziva dropped back down in the sitting position and then rolled onto her left side. Instantly, she felt relief.

The only thing the guards had removed was her gag. Wherever she was, they didn't want her to see anything, but they weren't worried about her calling out for help. *I won't waste my breath. I already know no one will come.*

Ziva had held on to a sliver of hope that Myla would've reached Alex, and he'd be her knight in shining armor, rescuing her from her captors. But as more time had passed, that sliver diminished. It was too late. There was no way he'd find her. She might not know exactly where she was, but she knew the countryside well enough to know there weren't any steep hills within two hundred miles from the town she'd been in.

She had anticipated death, which is why she'd dropped to her knees in the first place. Fighting them would've been futile and would've dragged out the inevitable. Or so she'd thought. Yet, she was still alive. She'd been trying to figure out why since they'd grabbed her.

Ziva played out each scenario in her head. If she'd been from a family with money, it was possible they'd hold her for ransom. Since she had no living family that was easily crossed off the list, so why would they bother keeping her alive? It didn't make sense.

If they'd believed her to be a virgin, they could hold

her and sell her. Men weren't coming here and paying good money for someone her age. They wanted the young beauties. Even if they had considered it, they would've been more delicate with their treatment. *What man, cruel enough to pay for a virgin, wanted damaged goods?*

Ziva had a hard time believing they thought she was innocent. Years ago, she made public she wasn't innocent. People of her culture didn't forget such things. *That was why I never married.*

That left only one thing. *They're going to torture me for information.* Her best guess: they'd seen her with Alex and were going to use her to flush him out. Make him reveal his hand that he's not a scum-sucking bastard like his father.

I'll die before I give up any information about Alex. Have I put him in danger? I did him an injustice before, and I won't make that mistake twice.

Her lips were dry and cracked from the gag. "Can I have some water?" She didn't expect an answer, but she had to try. If she were dead, she'd be no good to any of them. Trying again, she called out louder, "I'm thirsty."

To her surprise, she heard the sound of a key, and the door creaked open. Footsteps came closer to where she lay on the floor. Then she heard the door slam shut again, and the key turned. She was no longer alone. *Crap.*

Ziva felt a hand reaching behind her knees and another behind her back. Strong arms lifted her into the air. She was being carried off. *Hopefully not to be dropped on the floor again. My body is done with this.*

When she was placed down, she felt herself sink into the comfort of a soft bed. The cool silk sheets against her tattered body felt heavenly. Then she stiffened. A bed meant one thing. She wanted to scream, but she knew there was no hope.

Ziva was rolled onto her stomach. She held her breath as the duct tape was gently peeled away. The parts that had been in contact with her skin were tender and irritated. Moving her hands, she was about to rub them when she felt lips touch one wrist then the other.

She didn't move at all. Whoever was there wasn't speaking, and she was sure there was a reason for that. Still on her stomach, she felt hands untie the blindfold. Instantly the pressure was released, and she let out a heavy sigh. *Thank you, whoever you are.*

Ziva had to see who this was. As she rolled, a hand came up and covered her mouth. Her eyes widened, and her heart filled with joy. *Alex! What is he doing here?*

He put a finger to his lips to tell her to be quiet. Then he pointed to his ear. She understood. Her captors were listening to them. Ziva nodded.

Alex removed his hand from her lips. He stood by the bedside, and she could feel his eyes examining her. Each time he saw a bruise or cut, his jaw clenched tightly. Reaching her right hand up, she touched his cheek. With her eyes, she tried to let him know it was okay. That she was okay.

Alex covered her hand with his and closed his eyes, as though absorbing her loving message. When he opened them again, he continued to hold her hand, as he joined her on the bed. As though she were a china doll, he gently pulled her close and wrapped her in his arms. Her body melted into his. It didn't matter how sore she was, being close to Alex was where she wanted, no, needed to be.

She had so many questions for him, but they'd have to wait. All she knew was he was here with her. Ziva wasn't foolish enough to believe this would last. She lived in a reality that wasn't very pretty. Tomorrows were a gift, even the next few minutes weren't guaranteed.

Ziva turned her face toward his. His eyes held such sadness in them. He didn't appear to be hurt physically, but there was a pain that seemed as sharp as a knife to the heart. Alex didn't have to say the words. She could tell he knew something, and he not only couldn't tell her, but didn't want to, and it was tearing him up.

They had started with secrets and most likely would die with them as well. One thing Ziva refused to leave unsaid was that she cared about Alex very much. Knowing she couldn't utter the words, she had to show him.

Leaning closer to him her lips touched his. It was bittersweet. She knew if they were listening, most likely they were watching as well. Anything that transpired would be used against them later, so she had to keep it brief. *If we make it out of here, Alex. I promise no more secrets. No more lies.*

Alex closed his eyes and held her the entire night. He could tell she wasn't asleep either. His heart was breaking from the moment the guards delivered him to the room. He hadn't had a chance to look at her too closely when they'd first entered the house. The lighting had been dim, and she'd been too far off for him to see clearly.

Now in the bedroom, with the bright light overhead, he was able to see the dried blood on her legs and the bruise on her face. That was all he could see. He could only imagine what he couldn't see.

He wanted a basin of water or something so he could clean her wounds. It pissed him off that Rajani had let Ziva be treated so poorly. He had a feeling this was better than what could've taken place. If Rajani hadn't thought Ziva would be useful to obtain whatever she wanted, Alex was positive Ziva wouldn't be alive right now. *Why had they believed this was the only way to get me here? Why involve her?*

Nothing eased his mind. Rajani's words hadn't been an idle threat. He knew if he didn't comply, she'd have Ziva killed. Alex wasn't sure what Rajani wanted, but he knew he would say yes. *Even if it costs me my life, the answer will be yes.*

Rajani had told him all they had was one night. He knew the guards would come for him at some point, and his time with Ziva would be over. Once they took him from this room, he might never see her again. Never before had he felt such pain within him. Pain had surrounded him his entire life, yet this by far exceeded any.

Alex wasn't sure what he felt. He wasn't one who believed in love, especially after knowing someone for such a short time. This feeling wasn't lust because it wasn't his cock aching. It was an indescribable tightness in his chest. The thought of Ziva suffering or dying made him physically ill.

He didn't want to open his eyes as he feared seeing their reality. Yet, he needed to look upon her lovely face one more time. No matter who heard them, he needed her to know she was important to him. *More important than I could imagine.*

As his eyes opened, he saw the sun was rising as well. Since Bennett hadn't shown up during the night, it wasn't looking good. He'd written several books where characters were held hostage. Each time, rescue teams hit under the cover of darkness. *Hit hard. Hit fast.* All night he'd played out each scene. He knew exactly what he'd do if he were Bennett. Since he'd carried the duffel bag, he knew Bennett had the weapons needed to take out the guys in the towers. Long-range rifles would do the job easily. He'd seen the night-vision goggles stashed inside as well. If it were him, he'd take out the power and pick off the guards one by one. *Yeah, I've written this scene plenty of times.*

Since none of that took place last night, and he was still trapped in the room, he knew the window of opportunity was over. He'd have to be a fool to hit this place in the light of day. It was a well-armed fortress.

He'd counted more than a dozen men when he'd arrived. With Rajani here, he was positive there were two or three times that many. *Even if he could get in, they'd take us out long before Bennett found us. That's if he didn't get himself killed first.*

Knowing that a rescue wasn't coming helped him make his decision. When the guards came back for him, he'd go peacefully. It wasn't going to be a battle of strength that would save Ziva. It was one of wits. Alex needed to stall for as long as he could, negotiate Ziva's release, and agree to whatever Rajani wanted. *She holds all the cards. Somehow, I need to pull an ace out of my sleeve. I just hope she doesn't call my bluff.*

Alex didn't want to spend what little time he had left thinking about Rajani. He wanted every second to count. Raising himself up, he rested on his elbow. He wanted to look at Ziva's face and memorize every single inch. Her eyes fluttered open, and she smiled at him. It was the most amazing way to start the day. *If only all my days started with you in my arms. I can understand what Brice says. Lena is his home, his life, his purpose. And that is something I will never experience.*

Alex mouthed the words *good morning*. She responded likewise. He could see the concern in her eyes. Did she know what was about to happen, or was it just a reflection of his fears? He needed to find a way to tell Ziva this wasn't over. He would fight for them.

Reaching for her hand, he took it and placed it over his heart. Then he mouthed the words, *trust me.* Taking his hand, she placed it over her heart. With her eyes glistening, she nodded. *I do.*

It was all they could do, all they could share, yet it was more than he'd ever shared with another living soul.

All too soon, he heard the key enter the lock and the knob turn. He gave Ziva a wink and rolled away from her. Standing by the bed, he turned to the guard. "Let's get this over with."

The guard stepped aside, and Alex walked out the door. He couldn't bring himself to look back. If he did, she might see he wasn't as confident as he'd pretended to be. *I won't be coming back.*

The guards stopped at the bathroom and told him to freshen up. There was a shower and clean clothes waiting for him. Although it was needed, he wasn't out to impress Rajani.

Once again, he found himself in Rajani's office. This time she offered him a chair. She could offer him anything she wanted, but there was only one thing he wanted. Pissing her off wasn't going to help get it.

Taking the seat across from her, he said, "I have a lot of questions. Is this a two-way conversation today, or have you already made up your mind?"

She slid her glasses down, so she looked at him over them. "Does that mean you want to hear more about the arrangement between our fathers?"

Fuck no. I don't give a shit what those sick bastards promised. Alex knew he needed time. He also needed to gain her trust. *Although, hell will freeze over if you think*

I'll trust you. "I can't make a decision until I know how this all came to be."

"I thought I explained that last night."

"You didn't give me any details. I know my father was involved. What I don't know is what he got out of it." *Besides feeding his sick perverted needs and six children.*

"Oh. You want to talk money."

Money was never a driving factor for Alex, yet he knew it was for Rajani. He needed to meet her on what she valued. She looked at this as a business, no different than if she was selling makeup or any other goods. That proved how sick and deprived she was. *Beyond help.*

"Partly, yes. And what my father was committed to delivering in exchange."

"You don't strike me as someone who'd want to know all the little details about our arrangement."

"I can't make a decision without the facts, can I?" He held his voice in a professional manner that almost made him cringe.

"Tabiq is a very poor country. Although we have other sources of revenue, there is one that is most profitable. All it took was the right connection. My father had the resources available; he needed the connections to many people with money who'd be willing to pay for such resources."

Every time he heard women referred to as resources, he wanted to punch the shit out of her. He never would've thought he'd hear those words spoken by a female. It was worse than when a man said them. *You should be appalled at what is happening to the women in this country. Instead, you're sitting here, thinking of how you're going to keep the money flowing.*

Alex grew up knowing his father had no respect for women. He'd told his children women were all whores and were only good for one thing. How it was possible that neither he nor his brothers thought such things was beyond him. *Maybe it was because we had Sophie Barrington, who showed us differently.*

It was amazing that one woman had made such a difference in their lives. She was the mother of their friends. Yet, she'd always been there for them. When she said her door was always open, she meant it. The only things she'd ever shown the Henderson kids were kindness and empathy for their situation. Although she never said a negative thing about their father, her act of welcoming them into her home said she didn't like or trust him.

Ziva reminded Alex of Sophie. Although they were different in many ways, their selflessly kind acts touched others, even if they didn't realize it. *Everything I've done was for me, my own gain. This behavior has to stop. If I live . . . I can't continue to be that person. Otherwise, I'm chasing money like my father. I don't want to be anything like him. I don't even want to be his son.*

"How was that profitable for him?"

"We were able to obtain two million dollars from you for five nights with Ziva. Think about every time one of those rich men came to Tabiq. Who brought in revenue would depend on the cut. If James brought in a client, he and my father would each receive forty percent. The other twenty percent would be divided among the other partners. As you can see, it's advantageous to be the one bringing in clients. At eight hundred thousand dollars for each transaction, one could find themselves with a lovely little nest egg for hardly any work. It might be something you consider taking over. I'm sure a man like you knows people who might be interested in what we have to offer."

The hell I do. I don't associate with fucking assholes like that. He tried to keep his cool. Everything was riding on her buying into this. "I know people."

"Do you genuinely think I believe you're interested in taking over where your father left off?" Rajani crossed her arms and leaned back in her chair, staring at him.

Alex looked her straight in the eye. "I'm a Henderson. We like money. If you haven't noticed, unlike my brothers, I don't honestly work. I like to obtain my money in an unconventional way." *Just not the illegal shit you think I'm talking about.*

She arched a brow. "So you admit you weren't here to utilize our services?"

He needed to put some truth out there. "I told you before; I'm looking for my mother. My father told me where to look, and I have no intention of leaving until I meet her." The only truth was he wanted to meet her. James never spoke to them unless he had to. Usually it was about how they were a disappointment and how he wished they didn't exist. He'd never have told any of them anything personal and most definitely nothing about their mother. *Or mothers. Hell, all these years we thought there was only one. Not six. I'm not sure I can deal with more surprises my father had hidden from us. They keep getting worse.*

"Why would you want to meet her? She's nothing."

She's my mother, you bitch. "Does it really matter why I want to meet her? Or will it cost me another million dollars to do so?"

Rajani smiled. "Now you are beginning to understand how we work here. Good. Because if you're really interested in becoming a partner, you'll have to prove yourself first."

He didn't like the sound of that. "And how exactly should I do that?"

"Kill Ziva," Rajani said, staring him coldly in the eyes.

Like a punch in the gut, he sat straight up. "Let's get something straight. I'm not a murderer and fail to see how killing a woman proves anything to you. However, if anything happens to Ziva, there will be no further negotiations between us. Do you understand?" Alex growled out the words.

"I don't believe you're in the position to make any demands, Alexander."

"On the contrary, I'm the one who has the next generation of clients. If you want me to join as a partner, you will uphold my request."

"You think you're the only one with contacts?"

"Our reputation is well-known worldwide. Feel free to find someone else. If it's money you're after, I know where we can find it," Alex said, never taking his eyes from hers. He could see she was torn between her greed and ceding a portion of her control.

Rajani got up from her desk and paced slowly. It was the first time she seemed off her game. It was his opportunity to go in for the kill.

"It's time to raise the price as well. One million dollars is chump change for the people I know. I say we entice them with something more than what you've been able to provide."

She spun around and met his gaze. She was assessing him. Not turning away, he waited. The ball was in her court. "And what exactly do you think that would be?"

He had her. She was interested. "Let Ziva go, and we can talk. Nothing happens till I have proof she's returned to her town unharmed."

Rajani glared at him. "You're surprisingly a true Henderson. An asshole in business, just like James. But I'm like my father as well. We don't jump at one offer without considering all options. I'll have the guard take you to your room. Once I decide, I'll let you know."

Alex stood and headed to the door.

"By the way, Ziva is no longer on the premises. She hasn't been harmed . . . yet."

He didn't like her version of harmed. Alex had felt the welts, seen the cuts. As far as he was concerned, they'd already hurt her. Then again, he knew he and Rajani didn't see eye to eye on that.

Alex turned and shot her a warning look. "It damn well better stay that way." He didn't stay for her response. For once, he wanted the last word. All he could do was hope she agreed. If Ziva could get back to town, he knew Bennett would snag her, and she'd be safe. After that, Alex didn't care what Rajani did. *Kill me for all I care, but I'll never help you. If I do anything, it'll be to take you down and send you to visit your father and mine. Six feet under is exactly where you belong.*

Chapter Eleven

WHEN THE GUARDS took Alex away, she wanted to scream and beg them to take her instead. She knew what they were capable of, and she didn't want him to go through it. She knew her fate was already sealed.

All she could do was lie there and wait for him to return. When she heard the key in the door once again, she knew it hadn't been long enough. Sure enough, it was a different set of guards that entered. The looks on their faces said plenty.

She saw the duct tape and knew she was going somewhere. *Or to be disposed of.* Ziva always said she'd never go without a fight. Doing so with Alex somewhere, possibly within earshot, meant risking his life as well as her own. She'd never do that.

Getting off the bed, she walked to the guard, turned around, and placed her hands behind her back. Although she wasn't making a ruckus, the guard grabbed her arms forcefully, pulling them up and winding her wrists and hands together tightly. *I can only imagine what you would've done if I'd decided not to be so compliant.*

As before, the blindfold came next. The guards didn't want her to see where she was coming from, giving her hope they weren't about to kill her. *Dead girls don't talk.* This tidbit of knowledge wasn't enough to cause elation. Things could change very quickly.

As they made their way through the halls, she could hear someone talking in the other room. She tried to make out what was being said, or at least hear Alex's voice. All she heard was the faint sound of a woman's voice. *Please don't tell me they have more women prisoners here.* Although she wanted to call out and help in some way, there was nothing she could do. *I'm not even able to help myself.*

Ziva felt the butt of the rifle push against her back, reminding her to keep moving. She wasn't setting the pace. The guard who had her by the arm led the way. She knew he was taking his time, and it obviously had nothing to do with her safety or well-being. *Given how roughly I was thrown in the trunk, no one cared.*

Her traveling accommodations had improved as they tossed her into the backseat of a car instead. "Stay down and don't move. If I hear one word from you, I'll pull the car over and put a bullet in your head."

Ziva didn't have to be told twice. She knew they were itching to do just that, so what had prevented them? Could Alex have said something to get her released? *Released might be too strong of a word. I still have no idea where they're taking me.*

She was filled with questions that couldn't be asked or answered. All she could do was lie still and wait to see what happened next. Since she hadn't slept, she forced herself to relax so she could regain some strength. No matter what was in store, she needed to be both mentally and physically prepared.

Thankfully sleep did come. Although Ziva was haunted with thoughts about the girls, she still had an overwhelming feeling they were being taken care of. It was strange because all these years no one had ever lifted a finger to assist her. She'd have guessed it was Alex, but he was under lock and key. It couldn't be Myla because she was too young and didn't have a job to support them. *There's no one else, yet I feel as though they're better off, more than they've ever been. Maybe it's the hit on my head. I'm delusional. If I am delusional, I don't want to believe lying in Alex's arms last night was a dream. I've never felt so secure and at peace, which was ironic, given the truth of where we were. Yet in his arms . . . I felt protected.*

She knew it was out of her hands now. She could only hope what she felt in her heart was happening. If so, it was all worth it. *My life will not have been for nothing.*

Ziva heard the car horn blaring then the slamming of brakes, causing her to fly forward, ramming against the front seats before dropping to the floor. The guards cussed in their language about some idiot who had just cut them off. She heard a door open as a man shouted for the driver to move his vehicle. That's when she heard the sound of glass breaking, and then a loud thud.

She couldn't tell what was going on. She heard a gurgling sound from the driver. Then nothing.

Her hands were still taped behind her back, and she was awkwardly wedged between the seats with no way to maneuver herself into a defensive position. She was a sitting duck for whoever approached.

Ziva lay there, holding her breath. She could hear footsteps crunching, getting closer. It wouldn't be long before they found her.

Whoever it was, was able to stop the car and obviously take the guards out, so they weren't people she wanted to cross.

The back door opened and a man's deep voice bellowed, "Miss Gryzb, we'll have you out of here in a minute. We just need to secure the perimeter first."

They knew her name? And addressed her formally? Ziva knew from his accent he wasn't local. He didn't sound like Alex either. With all her studies of languages, she'd guessed the stranger was from a southern part of the United States. And she felt . . . relieved.

As promised, the man returned and lifted her from the car. He removed her blindfold first. "Who are you?"

"Doug Attwood. Here to rescue you."

She looked at him closely. He didn't resemble Alex in any way, so it probably wasn't a relative. This man had much lighter hair and looked like he'd seen some action. "How did you know I was in trouble?"

"I'll let Bennett explain the details. Right now, we have to get you out of here. It won't be long before someone makes a call about what went down."

Ziva looked by the passenger's door and saw one of the guards lying in a pool of blood. Then she turned and saw the driver hunched over the steering wheel. She assumed he was dead as well. Doug was right, if they didn't get out of here quickly, the locals would have a swarm of armed thugs ready to retaliate. She didn't know who Doug Attwood or Bennett were, but they seemed like a better option than staying where she was.

"Would you mind?" She turned her back to him so he could remove the duct tape.

"Don't move."

She could feel the cold steel of a blade brush against her skin as he cut the tape away. Within seconds, she was free.

"There are two SUVs that'll be on us if we don't move now," Doug said, grabbing her hand and dragging her away from the car.

"How do you know?"

"Bennett picked them up in his rifle's scope. He's good, but we'd prefer to avoid any more bloodshed if possible."

Ziva had to agree. She wasn't one who believed in taking a life for no reason. All these years she'd been able to avoid such action. *I'd like to live out the rest of my life in the same way.*

She slid into the passenger's seat of a Jeep as Doug slid into the driver's seat. He handed her a pistol and asked, "Can you shoot?"

Ziva shook her head. The only time she'd held a gun was on Alex, and that one hadn't been loaded.

"Damn. Well, those goons don't know that, so if they start shooting at us, shoot back. Maybe you'll get lucky."

That wasn't her goal. She wanted to hold them off but would do what she needed to. However, she'd be shooting above them. *Probably would even if I were aiming at them.*

Their Jeep sped away, and she held on to the roll bar as they hit bumps at high speed. The dust made it almost impossible to see if anyone was following. She assumed Doug was in contact with Bennett through an earpiece, because he was talking to someone she couldn't hear.

"Roger that. We'll be there in five."

She wasn't sure where *there* was, but they were heading in the opposite direction from her hometown. Whoever this Doug and Bennett were, she needed to make them understand she had to get back. The girls needed her. Myla needed her. *And I need them.*

"Just pull over and let me out. I can make it from here."

Doug didn't even look at her. "That isn't happening."

"Am I *your* prisoner now?" she asked sarcastically.

"We were sent to retrieve you and protect you. There is no way I'm letting you out of here so you can get yourself killed."

"If you want to help someone, I can give you the

name of a man who was held captive with me. He's still there." Ziva's voice cracked as fear for Alex came rushing through.

"You're first. He's next."

She hoped they were talking about the same person, but it didn't make any sense to her why they'd rescue her and not him. "You do know who I'm talking about, right?"

"Alex Henderson," Doug stated matter-of-factly, while they made a sharp turn.

"Right. You know you can't leave him there. I mean, you know who he is, so you know he's important."

The Jeep rounded one more bend, and she saw what they were rushing toward. There was a chopper waiting, and two men with some big guns standing there as well. *I hope they're expecting us.*

Doug slammed the Jeep into park and said, "Let's go."

She didn't hesitate and rushed to the chopper. Doug gave her a hand, helping her inside, then climbed in beside her. The two men did the same. The door was still open, and she could see the SUVs Doug had mentioned, pulling up beside his Jeep. Several men leaped out and raised their weapons. Shots rang out from inside the chopper before the men on the ground got any rounds off.

Ziva leaned back against the seat and closed her eyes. She didn't want to watch. Bloodshed was inevitable, but she didn't need to witness it.

It felt completely surreal.

This whole scene was happening all because of her. No life was worth taking over her. *I'm nobody important.*

It wasn't long before the chopper was out of range, and the gunfire ceased. Ziva didn't open her eyes. Her nerves were in overdrive. She'd always lived her life quietly and out of the spotlight. Now she was getting rescued, as though she was in a movie. Nothing felt real except the pain that still rocked her body.

"You're important."

She opened her eyes and looked at Doug. "What?"

"You said to go after Alex because he was important. So are you."

She'd forgotten all about saying that. "Not compared to Alex."

Doug turned and looked at her seriously. It was odd, his voice wasn't commanding, yet he had a way of talking that made her listen. "Your value is no different from any other human being. Don't put him or anyone else above yourself. Besides, I have a feeling Alex would disagree with you, since he's the one who sent for us."

That made no sense. Alex was in no position to orchestrate a rescue for anyone. This was a well-thought-out plan. It wasn't that she didn't believe Alex was capable of doing such a thing, but he'd been with her all night. He couldn't have been in communication with their team.

"I tell you what. Why don't you go get him, and let him tell me that himself?"

Doug smiled at her. "I'm sure he will."

The pilot said something to Doug and handed him a headset with a mic. He slipped it on. There wasn't much talking from Doug's end, but he obviously was getting more instructions. "Roger." Then he handed the headset back to the pilot. "Looks like you have some friends that are anxious to see you again."

"Friends?"

"Brice said he has a bunch of young girls that won't quiet down until they see you're okay."

Ziva let out a heavy sigh. She had no idea who this Brice guy was either. All she knew was these men had rescued her, and they were also keeping the girls she'd been protecting safe. *Good girl, Myla. You did what I asked.*

Knowing all hadn't been lost, she became teary. Sniffing, she said softly, "Thank you."

The words were so simple in comparison to the debt she owed them. She'd been prepared to pay the price with her own life. She wasn't, and never would be, prepared for it to happen to the others. They deserved a chance, and because of these strangers, they would get it.

"Miss, we should be thanking you. I heard what you've been doing here. Very impressive."

She shot Doug a puzzled look. "You must have mistaken me for someone else."

Doug shook his head. "Nope. You've changed the lives for six girls that we know of. If you think about the ripple effect, what you've done will continue, and eventually you'll see the healing of the country begin."

It was her dream, yet that's all she ever knew it would be. The saying that it only takes one sounded great, but in reality, one person couldn't combat the amount of evil in Tabiq. "I would like to hope so. It's not easy going—"

"At it alone?"

Ziva nodded. "This is the first time anyone has helped. But you're not from here. You'll leave, and we'll be faced with the consequences." *The wrath for escaping so publicly was going to end with heads rolling.*

"I don't believe the plan is to leave you or the others behind. I'm sure Brice will fill you in shortly. We're almost there now."

She looked out the window and off on a hill she saw another two choppers. These were guarded heavier than the one she was on. They looked military, but she didn't see any insignia on them. Looking back to Doug she asked, "Did the United States send you?"

He laughed. "No, ma'am. I served my time in the Marine Corps. Now the others and myself . . . freelance where needed."

She'd heard all about distinguished retired military men being paid for their specialties, doing unimaginable things. They had plenty here from all over the world. The guards she'd seen where she and Alex were held weren't originally from her country. Yet the two who took her away were. "You mean mercenaries?"

"This is not about money. It's about what's right." He met her gaze as though trying to convince her he spoke the truth.

It was hard to trust in people she didn't know, when it had been impossible for her to trust the ones she'd known all her life. Ziva knew there were other people in the world, wanting to do good. She'd never met them in person.

Not until I met Alex.

His heart was good.

"You didn't just find us on a map. Who brought you here?"

"Henderson."

"Alex?"

"Yes. And his brothers, Brice and Dean."

She was having difficulty getting used to one Henderson here. There were more? She wasn't sure Tabiq could handle it. *Unless they're all like Alex.*

"You're telling me his brothers are here, and you rescued me instead of Alex? I don't think they're going to be very happy to see me when we land."

"They all have women of their own. They wouldn't expect anything different if they were facing the same situation."

Women of their own? I'm not Alex's anything. We have a connection of some sort, but we're two different people. I'd never fit into his world, and he'd sure as heck never want to come live in mine. Telling that to Doug wasn't appropriate. Saying it to his brothers wasn't either. This conversation would be between her and Alex. *If we ever get the chance. Until I know you're safe, I won't be able to rest.*

Their chopper landed, and two men approached her. They had some similar features to Alex, but she would've guessed a more distant relation.

"You must be Ziva."

She nodded.

"I'm Brice, and this is Dean. Glad to see you made it here safely."

"I'll be happy when you tell me Alex is safe as well."

Brice turned to Doug. "Bennett?"

"In position," Doug replied.

"The others?" Dean asked.

"All within range. When we have the choppers in the air, we'll give the signal to go in." Doug's tone was so different than what he'd used when speaking to her. He was all business. She wasn't sure what their plan to extract Alex involved, but she was glad to see they had one.

"I want to go," Ziva sputtered out.

All three men said in unison, "No."

She knew it didn't make any sense, but she wanted to be there as he emerged. She wanted to run to him and wrap her arms around him. It wasn't just about holding him tight. It was about holding on to each other. For the first time since she was a child, she hadn't felt alone. Even though she knew it wouldn't be forever, she wanted every second they could have together so she'd have memories to last her a lifetime.

While the men went back to their discussion, Ziva

saw the girls rushing over from one of the choppers. There was nothing left for her to do here, so she made a mad dash to meet them halfway. There wasn't a dry eye as hugs were exchanged. Although she was still sore, their tight squeezes brought back the hope she'd lost. "I'm so glad to see you're all okay."

"Your Mr. Henderson made sure we were," Myla said.

Ziva was too happy at the moment to correct Myla. There had been so few times in her life that she'd felt this elated. She wanted to share in the joy with them. Yet, no matter how she felt at this moment, she couldn't be content until she was able to lay eyes on Alex and know he was safe as well. Only then would all be well. *And I can truly be happy. If only for a short time.*

ALEX HAD ONCE again been summoned to join Rajani. This time it was for a late dinner. He wasn't so sure about eating anything they were serving. The odds of her poisoning him was fifty-fifty.

Not having much choice in the matter since his escort took him to the dining room with an M-16 pointed at his back, Alex decided he might as well eat. *If I'm going to die, may as well be on a full stomach.*

The guard stood in the dining room with him, never taking his eyes off Alex. It wasn't like he was protecting anyone at the moment. Rajani was nowhere in sight. The food was getting cold, and he was positive this hadn't been part of her plan. How he hoped that meant Bennett had put a kink in whatever Rajani had in store for Ziva. *I need to know she's safe.*

The door finally opened, and Rajani entered, dressed in a long, red formfitting gown, slit high on one thigh. Her hair was pulled back, and he noticed she wore a flower behind one ear. *This better not be on my account, because it ain't going to fucking happen.*

She walked over and placed a hand on Alex's shoulder and asked, "Do you like what you see?"

He didn't look up at her. Instead, he replied, "Red is a bold color."

"Only someone very passionate and confident can wear this color, don't you think?" Rajani asked in a seductive tone. Alex wanted to hurl. Everything about her made him sick. The last thing he wanted was her touching him. No matter what, he would never physically hurt a woman. *If I could, I'd reach up and break every one of those fucking fingers. I don't want her near me at all. But until I know Ziva is safe, I have no choice but to play games.*

Rajani waved her hand in the air, dismissing the guard. He gave Alex a warning look before leaving the room. Her actions surprised Alex since she really had no idea if he was a man with honor. For all she knew, he was just like his father. *If I were, you'd last thirty seconds alone with me. If that long.*

She didn't take the seat at the far end across from him, which he'd hoped. Instead, she sashayed and settled herself in the seat beside him. "I hope you're . . . hungry."

Not for what you're offering. "Not really."

Rajani walked her fingers up his arm and touched his jaw. Turning his face, he had to look at her. He imagined men found her very attractive, until she opened her mouth and they heard the darkness in her heart. She disgusted him in every way possible. *When I look into those eyes, I'm reminded of my father. I'm not sure if either of you are even human, because no one with a soul could do what the two of you have done. Pure evil.*

"Maybe we skip dinner and move right to dessert then?"

"Actually, I'm hungry after all."

She removed her hand and said, "Disappointing. But since the guards told me you hadn't eaten a thing since you arrived, I think some nourishment would be wise. You'll need your strength for later."

Rajani, playing the sweet hostess, rose and served him as though he actually was her man and would be impressed by such pampering. It wouldn't matter if she danced on the table naked, he wasn't interested. Why was she doing that? She couldn't be interested in him. It was obvious he cared about Ziva. He knew damn well Rajani had been listening and watching. *Even that thought disgusts me, that something so heartfelt between Ziva and me had been monitored.*

He stuck his fork and knife into what looked like chicken, cut it, then brought it to his mouth. If it were poisoned, he'd know quickly. His only regret would be not knowing if Ziva was okay.

Alex continued eating, and Rajani kept her hands off him. He'd eat for hours if it accomplished that one thing. He'd cleaned his plate and was about to ask for more when he heard yelling in the hallway. Rajani rose from her chair. Alex didn't need to know the language to understand shit was going down.

The sounds of gunfire echoed through the room. Rajani headed for the door. Alex grabbed the knife from the table and in two long strides, he reached out for her. Pulling her back up against him, he said, "Not waiting for dessert?"

Rajani shouted something in her language, and the door burst open. Two guards stood there with their guns drawn. Alex took the knife and pressed it against Rajani's throat. He didn't want to hurt her, but right now she was all that stood between him and bullets.

He'd written this showdown in his last book. In his story, the guards glared at the hero, but there was no way in hell the hero would back down. It was a battle of wills, and the bad guys always lost.

Alex knew what he needed to do to play this out. "Tell your boys to drop their weapons, or I'll slice your throat." Words he would've written in his novel but never thought he'd utter himself. He hoped she wouldn't call his bluff, because he didn't think he could go through with it.

This wasn't one of his novels, and one of the guards pulled the trigger hitting Rajani in her leg, and grazing

Alex's thigh. *Fuck. All these bastards are crazy. Alex knew they were playing for keeps, and their lives didn't mean any more than his.*

"Let me go, or the next one will be through my heart and trust me, with that gun, it won't kill only me."

She hardly flinched when she was shot. There was no way she was joking. These men would shoot to kill, even if it meant her. *Well bitch, I guess we go down together.*

He pulled her closer and made sure the men saw the knife clearly. "Guess this is the end of our business arrangements."

The guard raised his gun, and Alex prepared for what was coming. He knew she hadn't lied. That caliber would go right through both of them at this close range.

At the last second, Alex turned quickly, so the bullet just missed them both. There'd only been one shot fired, yet both guards slipped to the floor. Looking from the dead guards, he saw Bennett standing there. He was holding his guns up with the silencer on them. He knew exactly who dropped those two guards.

Alex let out a heavy sigh. "That was too fucking close."

"Looked like perfect timing to me. So, who's this young lady?" Bennett asked.

Alex shoved her away from him and toward Bennett. "Trust me, she's no lady, and she's all yours. I wouldn't take my eyes off her if I were you. She's a fucking viper. I'll update you on the rest on our way out of here." There was nothing else he wanted but to see Ziva.

Bennett hadn't mentioned her. "Is she—?"

"Safe, sound and waiting for you."

"Then let's get the fuck out of here."

Chapter Twelve

Ziva stood alone on the top of the hill. Even though the girls all wanted to be by her side, she needed her space. Most of her life she'd wished to be surrounded by others, but right now, she needed to face this alone.

Her heart was racing as Dean approached her. *Don't bring me bad news. I can't handle it. I need him to be okay.*

"Mr. Hend—"

"It's Dean. And you can breathe now. He's on the chopper and safe."

Tears of joy poured down her cheeks. She went from wanting to be alone to turning and burying her face in Dean's chest. She felt ridiculous because they'd hardly spoken at all, yet here she was clinging to him and unable to let go.

"I don't know what I would've done if—"

"Don't. Don't think about it. He's fine," Dean said, rubbing her back to soothe her sobs.

"You don't understand. It's all my fault. If anything had happened to him, I'd never have forgiven myself."

"Ziva, my brother is a big boy. Trust me. This whole nightmare had nothing to do with you. He came here on his own and set the ball in motion. If anything, I'm sure he feels like shit for getting you involved."

Ziva pulled away and wiped her cheeks. "He shouldn't feel bad. All he wanted to do was find his mother. He should have the right to do that. This country, my country, is so . . . full of corruption, the good people are swept under the carpet, and no one knows they're there. Believe me, Dean, there are good people. They're too afraid to be seen. If they are, the government makes them disappear."

"My brother told us what you've been doing. The risk you take by doing it. I've never heard Alex speak of anyone so highly."

"He mentioned me?"

Dean nodded. "Let's just say he made it very clear that if anything happened to you, heads were going to roll. I'm glad to see you feel the same about him."

It seemed so weird talking to Dean about Alex when she and Alex hadn't had a chance to speak directly about each other. This wasn't just any guy talking to her; it was his brother. Knowing Alex had mentioned her to his family touched her heart. *I hope it was all good and not that I pulled a gun on him or broke into his room. Unless he hasn't figured out it was me.*

"I can't wait for him to get here."

She looked toward the sky, hoping to see a light or something, but all was dark. Not even a star or moon to light the way, as the clouds seemed to take on the somber evening.

"They're close."

"How can you tell? I don't see anything."

"Lights would make them a target. You'll be reunited very shortly."

She looked at Dean, who shot her a smile. It was the first time she saw any resemblance to Alex. *Those smiles. They're both kind. Who would've ever thought Hendersons were nice people? Definitely no one from Tabiq.*

Sure enough, she heard the sound of the chopper coming over the ridge. The only thing louder was her heartbeat. She wanted to run and leap into his arms, but there were multiple choppers, and she wasn't sure which he was on. She would wait impatiently. *Hurry up, Alex. I don't think my heart will hold out much longer.*

It hadn't been twenty-four hours since they'd seen each other, but it was what they hadn't been able to say as hostages that rushed to come out. Ziva had no clue what the words were going to be. She'd just sorted out what she felt herself. *We were brought together through a dramatic situation. How do we know if what we feel is real? It might be an adrenaline rush.*

Straining to focus her eyes, she saw a tall figure disembark one of the choppers and make his way toward her. Each step brought the figure clearer. *Alex!*

Unable to hold back, she dashed toward him. As she got closer, he opened his arms, and she leaped into them happily.

His lips claimed hers. It was a long overdue minute, filled with many unspoken words; the world around them could've ended and neither would've noticed. It seemed endless, yet ended all too quickly, as a voice from behind interrupted them.

"Hate to break up this reunion, but we have to get out of here before anyone comes looking for her."

Ziva thought they were speaking about her. As she looked over Alex's shoulder, she saw a man dressed in all black like Doug, but he was with a woman dressed in an elegant red gown, tugging along. Still, in Alex's arms, she asked, "Who are they?"

"That's Bennett Stone. He's in charge of the rescue team, among other things."

Ziva was glad to put a face with the name. She'd heard Doug talking to him, and from what she'd gathered, he was also the man behind the long-range rifle. *A good man to know.*

She turned her focus back to the woman Bennett had in tow. "And her?"

"Probably best I don't tell you."

Ziva shot her a warning look. They had much to work through. If they had been honest from day one, they might never have been held captive. Ziva wanted a fresh start. He'd asked her to trust him. That would require trust from both of them; it wasn't something that came easily to either one.

Her voice pleaded with him as she said, "No more secrets, Alex." He looked her in the eyes, and she hoped he saw the need for the truth.

Alex nodded. "She's the sick bit—person behind all the horrible things happening to the women in Tabiq."

"Her?" Ziva couldn't believe it. She looked prim and proper and maybe thirty-five years old, at most. There was no way she could order such brutality to the people here. Ziva said, "Please put me down." Alex did as she requested.

She walked over and stood face to face with the woman. "What's your name?"

She didn't answer the question but instead said, "How disappointing to see you're still alive."

Ziva knew then Alex hadn't exaggerated. She couldn't believe the woman's audacity. "My name is Ziva Gryzb. I've waited a long time for this moment. She curled up her fist, and with all her strength, brought her right arm up and rammed it directly into the woman's left cheek. The woman's head snapped back, her eyes rolled back, and she fell to the ground. "That's for all girls I couldn't save."

Ziva couldn't believe she'd physically assaulted someone. Bennett had a big grin on his face. Alex wasn't moving either. She went to check for a pulse when Alex stopped her.

"Leave her."

"Is she . . ."

"Dead?" Bennett answered.

Ziva nodded. She never wanted to hurt another human. *No matter what they've done. I want to be the best me*

I can be.

Alex pulled her close. "She's not dead, Ziva, just out cold."

"Nice right hook. I think you left a lasting impression on viper lady. She won't forget your name," Bennett said as he bent down, scooped the woman up, and placed her over his shoulder. "I'll go and pretend I care what happens to her. You two commence your reunion."

When Bennett was out of earshot, Alex lifted her off the ground, squeezed her tightly, and said, "You have no idea how happy I am to see you."

She choked out, "Not as happy as I am to see you."

"I say we take one of the choppers and debate this privately."

Her pulse raced for an entirely different reason as he slipped an arm beneath her legs and carried her away from where everyone else had been waiting. "Your brothers. They're waiting for you."

"Let them wait. Right now, you're the only person I need to see."

Alex placed her gently into the chopper he'd just disembarked. "Where are we going?"

Alex gave the pilot instructions. It was a place she'd never heard of. "We're heading to an island not far from yours, but far enough away not to be disturbed."

Since they weren't flying commercial, Alex bypassed the travel restrictions commonly faced when coming and going from Tabiq. It was a reminder that his name still carried power. Something she didn't have. It was something she didn't want to focus on now. If they only had a short time to escape from reality, she was going to grab that opportunity with both hands. *And make any happiness I find carry me through with some sweet memories later.*

"As long as I'm with you, any place is perfect." She found the island of Tabiq beautiful, but she didn't want to be there with him now. Someplace neutral was perfect. *And someplace private is even better.*

HE DIDN'T TAKE her far, only out of the reach from anyone wishing her harm. As they flew, Ziva slept snuggled in his arms. It was wonderful holding her quietly for hours. He dozed off himself. His body was tired, but he couldn't relax completely. There was too much he wanted to ask and needed to say.

When they walked down a lush green path, he held her hand so she didn't slip. He hoped she wasn't disappointed by not being at some fancy hotel with an ultra-soft bed. That wasn't his style.

He heard crashing water as they neared the site. He turned and peeked at Ziva, who smiled. *I guessed right.*

They turned the bend and came upon a waterfall that ran into a secluded pond. He'd found this location years ago by accident. He knew he'd return someday and purchased the small island right then. Unfortunately, the opportunity to return hadn't presented itself. *Until now.*

"Wow. This place is . . . beautiful." Her eyes opened wide as she took in the scenery.

Pulling her into his arms, he said, "Yes, you are."

She laughed. "I haven't had a shower in two days, and I look like I've been beaten. You're either tired or blind."

"There are other reasons that we can discuss later. I do agree; a shower sounds good." Letting her go, he pulled his shirt over his head and tossed it to the ground. Pointing to the waterfall, he asked, "Care to join me?"

Alex kicked off his shoes, removed his belt, jeans, and socks. Standing in his boxers, he waited for her to respond. By the curl of her lips, she contemplated his offer. Her eyes focused on his left thigh. *I'd forgotten about that.*

"What happened?" she asked, as she stepped over and touched the wound gently.

Ziva might've been trying to soothe the pain, but she created an entirely different ache within him.

"Just a graze. Nothing to worry about."

"You were shot?"

"No. Rajani was shot. This is just a flesh wound. Actually, cleaning it in the water is probably a good idea." Not that he thought she needed any encouragement to join him, but he didn't want to stand there talking about anything right now. He felt his cock begging to be released. Alex wanted her but didn't want to rush her.

She looked as though she doubted what he told her. Then he ran his fingers over the injury and said, "See, it's fine." Of course it hurt like hell, but he wouldn't admit that. If he were home, he would've gone to his brother Logan to get a few stitches. Until she brought it up, he had no idea how bad it was. *Graze may be an exaggeration.*

She must've bought it because she turned and looked at the water. "Is there anything in there that bites?"

He laughed. Here he was trying to be romantic, and her concern was for creatures that might be lurking around. "Not that I've experienced before."

Ziva turned to him again and said, "So you've brought other . . . people here before?"

She almost sounded jealous. No one had ever cared who he was with or when. It was odd, but he liked it. "No. I've only been here alone. And now with you."

She smiled as though that's what she'd been waiting to hear. He watched as she pulled off her T-shirt and removed her shorts. She wasn't one who wore fancy lace bra and panty sets. Ziva was practical, even in the choice of her undergarments. Both white cotton. *Would've shocked me more if you were wearing a thong.*

Alex saw various cuts and bruises along her body. She'd been put through hell these last two days. He wanted to hold her and tell her it'd never happen again. That was in the past, and he didn't want to bring it up. Not now. They both needed healing and not only physically.

He walked past her and entered the water. It was cool but not cold. He went to the waterfall side where it was more than chest deep. Turning, he watched Ziva stick her toe into the water to check the temperature. *Or to see if anything besides me wants to take a nibble.*

She surpassed everything he expected: touching the water with a single toe, rushing in and diving under the water, and coming up beside him. When she stood, he wished he were the water droplets clinging to every inch of her body. Dropping, he submerged completely then came back up.

"Alex, do you see those purple flowers growing along the edge? It's lavender. Do you think you can get me some?"

"I'd rather stay here with you, but your wish is my command." Alex wasn't going to admit he couldn't refuse her anything. He wasn't ready to relinquish that power.

Climbing along the edge of the waterfall, he grabbed a large handful and brought it to her. She took one of the stems, pulled the flowers off, rubbed the flowers between her hands, then rubbed her hands on her arms and upper body. A sweet aroma filled the air. Finally, she ran her hands through her hair and dove under the water to rinse off. When she popped up beside Alex all he could think was how damn good she smelled. *Good enough to eat.*

Ziva reached out and took another stem, rubbing her hands together once again. This time, after rubbing the flower briskly between her hands, she brought her hands up to glide over his arms and chest. "Turn around please."

He didn't want to as her hands felt amazing on him. But she was enjoying it, so he wasn't about to stop her. Alex allowed her to clean him just as she had herself. It was very intimate. After he'd rinsed off, he tossed the remaining flowers onto the shore. They could use them again later. *Right now, I want one thing. To hold and kiss every inch of your lovely body that's been teasing me since you undressed.*

He pushed past his own desires and remembered she'd been through hell and back. They also had a lot to discuss. Things she deserved to know. He took her by the hand and led her away from the pond to a bed of soft grass that was perfect for sitting. *All the comforts of nature.*

"I figured you might want to talk."

Ziva stopped dead in her tracks. Alex turned to face her, expecting to see concern or seriousness. Instead, she had a wild look in her eyes. She gave his hand a tug, encouraging him to come back to her. He was more than willing to oblige.

"Can't we *talk* later?" Her voice was throaty with need. She went up on her tip-toes and still couldn't reach his lips, so he bent to give her access. The kiss was better than the one they'd shared before. This one started off hot and explosive.

She parted her lips, and his tongue entered her mouth, twisting around hers, teasing and letting her know what was to come. Ziva took all he offered and then took control, entering his mouth and claiming all of him as well. When he pulled back, she clung to him, drawing him back to her.

Alex was on fire. His cock throbbed with need, and

every cell in his body wanted to touch her. *I need to taste every sweet inch of you.* Nothing would stop him now. They wanted and needed each other. As his kisses deepened, his tongue filled her mouth again, and her body melted against his. She began to explore, running her hands over his chest and biceps; his muscles tightened everywhere her fingers made contact.

He continued kissing her, making his way across her jaw and down her neck. "I've wanted you in my arms since the day I met you."

He felt her shudder as his lips moved farther down. "I know." Ziva's voice was barely a whisper.

His tongue darted out, licking from her collarbone to her breast, his fingers unhooking her bra while his tongue continued to trail to her cleavage. Her nipples were hard as though impatiently waiting for him to give them the needed attention. As he looked at them, she arched her back, offering herself to him. "I want you so much, Alex. Please, don't tease me. I need—"

"I won't tease you. I've wanted you for so long."

His cock ached to be released from its confines. He felt her hand slip inside the waistband of his boxers, and her fingers wrapped around him. When he tried to pull her hand away, she gripped him tighter.

"I want to touch you. All of you."

He let go of her hand, and she knelt in front of him. With her free hand, she pulled his boxers down. Her head was only inches from the tip of his cock.

"I've wanted—" She didn't finish her sentence, and

before he could say anything to her, her tongue touched the tip of his hard cock. *Oh shit.*

"Ziva."

"Alex, I want to . . . taste you."

He couldn't utter a word if he tried as her tongue darted out and licked the tip of his cock again. He'd wanted her so badly already; it was killing him to hold back. Adding to the sweet torture, he brushed her long, wet hair away from her face and watched her open her mouth and take him. She paused for a second, and he thought she'd changed her mind. That was fine with him. He never wanted her to do anything she wouldn't enjoy. But then she twirled her tongue around his cock and hungrily sucked and stroked him.

"Oh, God. Ziva, that feels so good." A groan rumbled through him as he fought to hold control. Each stroke caused his body to tense. Her tongue pressed firmly against his cock, licking his length then back to the tip, again and again, almost dropping him to his knees.

His blood pounded with raw need, all because of her sweet mouth. Ziva knew how to take him to the brink of no control yet hold him there without releasing. It was heaven and hell all in one.

Her rhythm became more aggressive with each stroke. Her own moans vibrated against his large cock as she took him deeper.

He knew he couldn't hold back much longer. Pulling away he said, "I'm not ready for this to end, so you have to stop now."

Alex dropped to his knees and helped her out of her panties. Then he took her hand and had her lie on the grass. He wished he'd brought a blanket or towel, but thankfully the grass was soft.

Alex looked into her gorgeous, dark eyes. "I get lost looking into them."

"Into what?"

"Your eyes."

He couldn't bring himself to tell her, but she'd stolen his heart. He couldn't express it in words, but he could show her as she'd shown him. Alex needed to touch her, give her the pleasure she'd given to him. *That and so much more.*

Alex brought his hand up and caressed her breast, her moans growing deeper, as he rolled a nipple between his fingers. He took the other one between his lips and sucked teasingly, flicking it with his tongue. He felt her tremble beneath him, and he wanted her wrapped around him. He couldn't cave to his own desire. Alex wanted her to lose control, and he wanted to watch her. Only then would he satisfy his own needs.

Reaching a hand between her legs, he felt how wet and ready she was for him. His finger slid between her folds, up and over her clit. Her legs jumped. She was so responsive to him; it only fueled his own desire even more.

"Please, Alex. I want you."

"And you'll have me, my sweet." Inserting his index

finger deep inside her, he brought his thumb up to circle her clit. He could feel her warmth inviting him, begging him for more. *So wet. So warm. For me.*

Alex couldn't get enough of her body and how it trembled at every touch. She quivered as he slipped his finger inside her again and again. Her dark eyes met his. "Soon, my sweet. Just enjoy it."

Breathlessly, she begged, "Alex, I can't wait . . ."

He entered her again and again, and she cried out in pleasure.

"Please . . . I—"

He knew she was close and increased the rhythm until her body jerked violently, and he felt her powerful release grip his finger.

"Yes. Oh, Alex, yes!" Her cries of passion echoed through the valley. He continued to stroke her with his fingers, slowly until her body began to settle.

His cock ached when he realized he hadn't brought any condoms with him. His reason for traveling to Tabiq hadn't been to have sex. If anything, it was to avoid it at all costs. Now he could kick himself for not putting one in his wallet. "Fuck."

Ziva looked up at him. "What's the matter?"

He could tell from her expression she thought it was something she'd done. "My sweet, I don't have any protection with me."

She relaxed some with his response. He, on the other hand, felt anything but relaxed. His cock was begging for release.

Ziva reached down between his legs and took hold of him. He didn't need any more torture than he already had. "Please, Ziva, we can't."

"Alex, I know my cycle. I'm safe."

Those were words no man ever believed or shouldn't anyway. They'd trapped so many men in unwanted relationships. But Ziva wasn't that type, and with her, he didn't feel trapped. From day one, he felt she could read his soul. They hadn't spoken many words to each other, apart from the day she took him to the prison. Yet here he was. With her. Tasting her. *Wanting* her. What surprised him the most was, he felt more comfortable with her than he did with anyone else. He never knew it would be so easy with someone. So quickly. Trapped was the last thing he felt when he was near her.

Looking at her, he knew she was serious, and he didn't care if she became pregnant. Until her, he wanted to spend his life alone, unattached. Home wasn't a place he wanted to be. It was just an address. He called her *my sweet* because that's who she was when he thought of her. *Nothing but sweet. And mine.*

He hadn't realized he was smiling until she mentioned it. "What are you smiling about?"

Alex would tell her, later. "Just admiring the view," he said instead. *Still true.*

She smiled at him, as she pulled him to her. "Then admire me closer."

He paused and looked into her eyes one more time and knew he was lost. He saw his own desire matched with hers.

He didn't want to take his eyes off her, and she seemed the same. As he buried himself deep inside her, he captured her lips with his and mumbled her name into her mouth. Their moans blended as they became one. Once he knew she'd adjusted to him—and his size—he slowly began to move inside her. *My sweet, you feel amazing.*

He started slowly at first, but she met him with her hips, encouraging him to take her deeper, faster. As their bodies came together, again and again, it was like nothing he'd felt before. This was far more than a physical act. It wasn't fucking. This was making love to someone. A feeling he'd never experienced before. An emotion he thought he was incapable of having.

Overtaken by the need within him, he began moving faster and deeper; her moans grew louder with each thrust. He gripped her hips and met her again and again. He could feel her body tense beneath him as she rocked with a second release. When she clenched around him, he lost what little control he had. Plunging one last time into her, he shuddered with his release.

They lay holding each other, panting. He couldn't imagine having *sex* again with anyone else, knowing how amazing it was with someone you . . . cared deeply about.

Alex wasn't ready to say love. He had no clue what that word truly meant. He'd heard it used by so many people that it had lost its meaning. Yet, holding her tenderly against him now, he couldn't think of any other word that explained what he felt.

He'd promised her they'd talk later. *That's what tomorrows are for. Right now, I want to enjoy what we shared. Maybe again in a few minutes.*

"I didn't know, Alex. I didn't know it could be like this. It was . . . so amazing," Ziva said breathlessly.

"I didn't know either, my sweet." *I truly didn't.*

Chapter Thirteen

Ziva could stay on this island forever with Alex. It was secluded and had everything one could ask for. There was an abundance of fruit trees and fresh water. The only thing it lacked was a proper bathroom. That was where she drew the line when it came to being an outdoors type.

"Alex, I'd love to stay here, but I need to go back. Myla and the other girls need me."

He lifted a hand and stroked her cheek with gentle tenderness. "I know. We should talk first."

Ziva agreed. There was a lot she needed to explain to him. "I'm really sorry that . . . well there's a lot I'm sorry for. Maybe I should start at the beginning."

"You don't have to apologize."

"I do. Please let me explain everything. It's important that you understand why certain things happened." Alex nodded. "My childhood was a good one to a certain age. When I grew older, my father explained to me what happened to some of the women here, things that were out of his control. He hid me away for a few years. It was the only thing that saved me from the fate of the others, well, and that we lied upon my return. Others like my sister, Isa."

"I'm sorry. I heard she disappeared when you were very young."

Ziva didn't know how he knew that. It was many years ago, and she never spoke about it. "How—?"

"Bennett. He does his job well. Sorry."

"Don't be. I wish he could tell me what happened to her. I could have closure."

"I'll ask him. But I can't make any promises. Although, I wish I could." Alex reached out and held her hand.

She knew he would do anything if she asked. Ziva wouldn't take advantage of that. "Thank you. Why I'm telling you this is so you understand why I did what I did. Your father, James, has a name everyone in my country knows. He was feared like no other. I know he was your father, but he was a very evil man. He had no love in his hear for anyone."

"Not even his own children," Alex said softly. Sadly, his statement didn't surprise her. He needed to remind himself that the Henderson clan wasn't the only ones who suffered at the hands of James.

"When I heard you were here, I needed to know why. When you went to the same hotel James went to all those years ago, I had to try to stop you. Then I saw you talking to the manager. He is the one who makes all the arrangements with the men and brings them the women.

The manager is just like James. Cold and evil."

"Agreed."

"I was watching you. Waiting for you to make a move so I could stop you from acting on your . . . what I thought was your sick, immoral behavior. I needed to know for sure, so I broke into your room and—"

"That was you?" Alex had a look of total surprise on his face.

She had a sick sense of pride that she'd been able to pull that off, and he never suspected her. Also, an overwhelming sense of guilt that she'd invaded his privacy. "I wanted to find proof of what you were doing. I thought if I could get the proof and post it on the Internet, your good name would be ruined, and you'd have to stop. I know it was naïve on my part, but I was desperate to stop you."

"My good name? I'm not sure you know anything about me," Alex teased.

"I researched you. Well, what I could find on you. There really isn't much. I'm not sure you have a job, but then again, I suppose with a Henderson bank account, you don't need one."

"I have a job. When you're done, I'll tell you about it."

"Sounds interesting. I broke in and found the weapons in the closet. I knew you were up to no good. But I had a feeling there was something good in you. That is why I took you to the prison. I thought I could scare you toward the right path."

Alex laughed. "You're barely five feet tall and you took me to a prison to intimidate me. Don't you think you should've been afraid of what I was going to do to you? I mean you found all kinds of weapons, and you thought I was like my father. I'm not sure you'd make a very good spy."

Ziva wrinkled her nose. "Really? And you think you would?"

"Well, yes. Everyone, yourself included, believed I was just like James. It all would've worked out if someone hadn't broken into my room and taken Myla. Oh yeah, also came back with a gun and tried to muscle me. By the way, don't ever pull an unloaded weapon on someone. No more guns for you, period."

Ziva laughed this time. "I couldn't hit the side of a barn if I tried. You would've been safe either way."

"Definitely no more guns."

"Well, it got your attention."

"My sweet, your beautiful face had my attention."

She wished he'd take her seriously, but his words warmed her heart. Ziva loved hearing him call her, *his sweet*. "I'm not as defenseless as you think."

"Oh, I know. I was there when you knocked Rajani out cold."

"I've never hit anyone in my life, so I was shocked. But that was years and years of fear and hatred coming to the surface all at once. What do you know about her? Was she really behind all the evil here?"

"I only know what little she taunted me with during

my not-so-lovely stay. My father and hers started this human trafficking business many years ago. Maybe even before my brother Brice was born. When her father died, she took over the family business. She hoped I'd be interested in doing the same."

"How could she think you'd be interested in such a thing?"

"How did you think I was like my father?" Alex gave her a wink. "I'm that good."

Ziva rolled her eyes. "Oh, please. I have you figured out now."

Alex arched a brow. "Really? Then tell me, what do I do for a living?"

She had no clue. "I don't know. Maybe nothing but sit home and watch movies," she teased.

"I do sit home a lot, but I travel mostly. What I'm going to tell you, no one knows. Not even my family."

"You're a spy?"

Alex chuckled. "Only in my head. Or maybe, should I say, only on paper. I'm an author. I write espionage books. You know, terrorist and drug lords and all types of crime stories."

"You're joking, right?"

"No. Why, what's so funny about that?"

She looked him up and down. "The way you handled things when we were captured. You were so calm and cool. Like you'd done that before. But in all honesty, I saw the storm brewing in your eyes, even though you acted calmly."

"Nope. Just wrote scenes like that before. It worked in the books, so I figured might as well try it in real life. But yes, there was a storm brewing, I realized how truly evil and sadistic Rajani and her muscled minions were. Greed is a powerful motivator to people like them."

Ziva's eyes widened in shock. "Are you telling me you risked our lives based on what you thought worked well in a book? That is the craziest thing I've ever heard. If I'd have known then—"

"Did my plan work?"

She studied him for a minute. He was cocky, but he was right. It had worked. They both made it out safely, and he got the bad guy. *Or woman.* "You got lucky. Life is not a book. Trust me. I've read so many with the happily ever afters. The happy endings are pure fiction."

"It doesn't have to be that way, Ziva."

She met his gaze. He wasn't offering anything, and it really didn't matter. She knew where she belonged, and he didn't fit. "Alex, don't try to write a chapter that won't fit in the story. Some books just end. You only have to enjoy the story while you're reading it. That's all."

Surprisingly, Ziva didn't want it to end, but she understood the truth. It must. Going forward, pretending any differently would be lying to each other. *I'm done hiding and pretending. I want to keep it real.* She didn't know what her life would look like. The policemen who had taken her had to work for the police department in town. She would be known here now. *What will I do?*

"What are you saying, Ziva?"

"That we can't have it all, Alex. This isn't one of your stories."

"I know that, but what we have, it's good. You can come back to Boston with me, and we can give it a shot."

Oh yeah, that's what every girl wants to hear. "Alex, I don't belong in that world, any more than you do in mine. We both know that. And besides, I have work I have to continue in Tabiq. You may have taken out the head, but our government is full of people waiting to step in and take Rajani's place. I have to be there to make sure someone speaks out against it."

"You can do that from Boston. There is no reason why you need to risk your life every day," Alex said.

"Yes, there is. This is my home. My people. It's what *I* do, Alex."

She could see he was putting the pieces together and starting to see things from her point of view. Ziva hated being right this time. With all her heart, she wished there was another way. Leaving would cause such pain with worry and him staying ... well, he'd hate it. *Who wouldn't? Tabiq is a god-awful place. But it's my home.*

"I understand," Alex said softly. "Don't think for a minute that I agree with you. We'll find a way to make this work. I'm not giving up on us."

Her eyes began to tear up. "I don't want you to let me go either, Alex. But it's what is best for both of us. Stop it now before it hurts too much." She knew it was already too late on her part, but she hoped he'd be able to go back to Boston and continue with his happy life. That's all that mattered. *Please be happy, Alex.*

"I wish we could stay here until we worked this out, but the chopper's approaching. This conversation isn't over."

They quickly dressed, and she wanted to respond but didn't. He wasn't joking. He'd drop it for now, but she knew he wasn't going to leave Tabiq without finishing it. Once they were dressed, he took her by the hand, and they made their way back to the helicopter.

He might think this was easy for her, but that was far from the truth. She had never imagined feeling as she did in such a short amount of time. He made her feel things she'd read in books, yet here she was telling him it wasn't real. She knew differently. Ziva's heart was breaking, and she was doing it to herself. Not because she wanted to, but because she had to. She wouldn't allow herself to say the words. Nor think them. It was already painful enough.

It might not seem over, but it has to be. For your sake, as well as mine.

"ALEX, ARE YOU even listening?" Brice asked.

Alex couldn't afford the distraction of Ziva right now. "Yeah. What were you saying?"

"You seem completely distracted. I'm surprised Ziva isn't with you," Dean chimed in.

He didn't want to talk about her right now. It wasn't time for him to deal with what he felt or didn't feel for her. There were more important things on the agenda right now. "Let's stay focused. Where's the manager now?"

Brice replied, "As I had *just* said, Bennett and Doug picked him up from the hotel. He and several of his men are being detained until the proper authorities arrive. This is a very complicated situation; the government isn't supportive of our assistance. We understand why, as it jeopardizes their significant source of revenue."

"We can't let these bastards continue," Alex barked back.

"Alex, there is only so much we can do legally," Brice stated.

"Hell, we've crossed that line already. I want this entire operation shut down. I'm shocked you don't feel the same way."

Brice's jaw clenched. "I'm going to let that comment slip for the moment and chalk it up to stress on your part. But don't think for one minute that any of us condone what has taken place here. Whether we like it or not, this fucked-up country is part of who we are."

"What are you talking about?" Alex demanded.

"We're American and Tabiqian," Brice said plainly.

He hadn't thought about it like that. Alex had linked this place with his mother only. Never had he considered this part of his heritage. Most people were thrilled to learn of their roots. For the Hendersons, not only had they learned their father played a major role in making this country what it was today—corrupt—but he did it to a place where his own children, his flesh and blood had come from. *Our people.*

"I hate that asshole!" Alex growled, wishing he'd said it just to himself.

"Who, the manager?" Dean asked.

"James Henderson," Alex replied. "All these years, I wanted to know more about him, thinking if I did, I'd understand why he was so fucking cruel to us. Instead, I find more skeletons in the Henderson closet than I could wri . . . imagine. I am a fool for thinking there was anything good in that man."

Alex couldn't believe he almost said the word write. No one but Ziva knew, and he wanted to keep it that way. It just hit him why. All this time he'd been trying to distance himself from being a Henderson. He'd published his books under a pen name and lived most of his life through that alias. So why had he felt comfortable telling Ziva, but not his own family? *Maybe because I don't want to be a Henderson. I want to be anyone but a Henderson.*

"You're no fool, Alex. We all face the same issue. James Henderson did only one thing in his life that was worth anything."

"What's that, Brice? Die?" Alex asked.

Brice shook his head. He walked over and placed a hand on Alex's shoulder. Giving it a squeeze, he said, "He gave us each other. Together we're going to find our mothers and help Tabiq become a place our children and grandchildren can one day be proud of. It's not easy, but we need to remember we're *not* our father, and we never will be."

Alex met Brice's eyes. He saw his own fears and insecurities in them. Then he looked at Dean and saw them there as well. Alex was far from alone in how he felt. Brice was right. They were powerful men who could change the world for good or bad if they stuck together.

"I've spent a long time trying not to be a Henderson. Maybe it's time to change how people view the name, because it will no longer define me. Hell, how *I* view the name."

"Sounds good. I'm in. What's the first step?" Dean asked.

Alex almost laughed. Dean was fearless and ready for any challenge. *One day you'll learn to ask first, then agree.* "For me to start being a Henderson."

"Didn't know you weren't," Dean said.

Brice nodded. "I know what you mean. But it's like any other business, it's not who you are, just what you do."

"What the hell are you talking about, Brice?" Dean asked puzzled.

Alex shot Brice a look. "All these years, you knew?"

"I may have seemed not to care, but I was always watching out for you guys. Had to make sure Dad didn't reel any of you in."

"Damn it, Brice. You could've told me."

"I figured one day you'd tell us."

Dean, aggravated with their banter, demanded, "Will

one of you tell me what the hell you're talking about?"

"We're talking about what Alex does for a living," Brice replied.

"Travel the world and vacation all the time from what I see." Dean laughed. "Real hard work."

"I do travel for business. I'm an author."

"No way in hell," Dean said, shaking his head. "You mean it. You wrote a book."

"I've written twenty-two books so far."

Dean ran his hand through his hair in total bewilderment. "What the fuck is wrong with me? Brice is a scientist. Logan, a neurosurgeon. Shaun, a financial wizard. Zoey, a self-taught pianist and composer. And now you're a published author. Where the hell is my talent?"

Both Brice and Alex laughed. "When it comes to business, you know how to build them. None of us thought you could save Poly-Shyn, but you did. Hell, you not only saved it, you surpassed what Dad had been able to do. And legally, too. We all would've ditched the company for pennies. That would've been a huge mistake."

Dean shook his head. "When I get home, I'm going to sit back and think about my talent. Maybe I'm a . . . singer or an actor. Fuck that. I'm a savvy businessman."

"Oh, thank God. If you'd decided to become a singer, the Henderson name surely would never recover," Alex joked.

It was refreshing to share a few laughs together. Especially after the ordeal they'd been through. Brice was right. None of them were alone. It was time to stop acting like they were. Although he didn't want to spoil the mood, he needed to get back to why they were meeting in the first place.

"Getting back to the manager. Did they get anything good out of him when they interrogated him?"

"He detailed. We found a ledger that held every girl's name, and also the bastards who paid for them," Brice said. "We have the names of our mothers, but not their whereabouts. Bennett and Doug are working on that as we speak."

Brice handed him the list. He scrolled to the name listed by his. Alex's heart raced. All this time had passed, and he now had a name. *Nikolet Maadi, my mother.* He scrolled through all their mothers' names. Zoey's popped out at him. *Teetta Maadi.*

"Brice, did you—?"

"Notice the last names? Yeah. And it's confirmed. Your mother and Zoey's were sisters." Brice replied nodding grimly.

"Guess we know where your artistic genes came from," Dean added.

"Dean," Brice growled. "It also means two sisters were taken from that family. Two. Can you fathom that?" No doubt this was more personal to Brice, given he also was a parent. When he met Brice's eyes, it was confirmed. His jaw twitched and his fist clenched. Then his focus returned back to his mother and her parents.

My grandparents. All their lives were hell. Nothing I ever say or do will change that. Or can ever repay the debt owed. Alex couldn't stop staring at the list. It was what he'd wanted since he was a small child, old enough to know a piece of him was missing. Now he had the name. He was elated, but something seemed to be missing. *Actually, someone. Ziva. I need to share this news with her. Celebrate with her.*

He was used to being alone. Surely he didn't *need* to share this with her. All he needed was to get back to Boston and settle right back into his normal way of living. *Just need some time and distance.*

"There's more that you don't know," Dean said.

Alex wasn't sure his head could handle anything else. "Make sure it's good news."

"We first thought Logan's mother had died giving birth to him. The information was incorrect."

He'd forgotten all about that. It would've been a blow to Logan. He'd always been so damn serious and uptight, but Alex hadn't been fooled either. Out of all of them, he was driven the most by his emotions. *Guess that's why he's the doctor and we're not. You have to save everyone.* "Have the others been told what we're doing here?"

Brice shook his head. "Not yet. We wanted to get all the facts first. I'd like to ensure the women are still alive before we update them."

"No matter what, it's going to be a shock. I wouldn't wait too long. I know how I felt being left out of the loop, Brice. Even now I believe there are things you know that you're not telling us."

Brice gave him a blank stare. It wasn't the answer he wanted. He'd have liked Brice to deny it and say there was nothing left unsaid.

"Is it about our mothers?" Alex asked.

"No. And not something anyone needs to worry about." Brice turned and headed toward the door. "If you don't mind, I'd like to say goodnight to my wife and kids before it gets too late."

Brice didn't wait for a response and left; Alex and Dean stared at each other. "That was strange."

"No. That's Brice. He's holding back something he thinks is in our best interest. I say we find out what the hell that is when we get back to Boston."

"Alex, I'm all in as long as you don't put me in one of your books."

He laughed. "If I do, I'll make sure to portray the character as a nice guy so no one will know it's you."

"Can you make me a few inches taller too? I seemed to have also gotten screwed out of the tall gene," Dean added jokingly.

"While I'm at it, I'll make you good-looking."

"Since we're both stuck sitting here with nothing to do, why don't we grab a beer?"

"Beer sounds good. I know just the place."

It was a place Ziva had taken him on their way back from the prison. It had been the first time either of them had let their guard down.

They headed out the door when Dean added, "Great, and you can tell me all about you and Ziva."

Alex didn't want to talk about her. Not to Dean or anyone else. "I have a few other topics I think we should discuss instead."

Dean laughed. "That bad, huh? Don't worry. You'll figure it out. Just takes us Hendersons a bit longer to get it through our thick skulls."

"That's an understatement." He wasn't going to argue with Dean. Hendersons were difficult people to love. It took special people to put up with them. *At one point I really thought Ziva may have been that person for me. But she's made it clear we won't have anything. I wanted solitude. Looks like I'm going to get it.*

Chapter Fourteen

She had so many mixed feelings about it all. She wanted to believe this cabin that had once been her safe haven wasn't needed any longer. That Tabiq would turn around. It was a beautiful dream and one she believed in, yet it was going to take time. *A lot of it. Greed is a disease that consumes and can be terminal.*

That was exactly how she looked at Tabiq right now: it was sick. James Henderson had been a major player in starting the problem, but it was the poverty of the people that made the money more attractive. If something didn't take its place, she feared the problem would return with a vengeance.

That didn't mean she didn't appreciate Alex and the others for shutting things down temporarily. In less than a day, the word had spread like wildfire. There wasn't a place you could go without hearing murmurings about Rajani and other notable players being under lock and key. Although people seemed to have relaxed somewhat, she knew they hesitated for the same reason she did.

With the crooks not in charge, everything started to

fall apart quickly. Their so-called police department was no longer in control because they weren't on anyone's payroll. So far, an outbreak of mayhem hadn't taken place. She noticed more people walked the streets. She still hadn't seen children outside playing or teenage girls come out of hiding. When that happened, she would know things had turned around for good. Until then, everyone would be extremely cautious and watchful.

Ziva wished she could be oblivious to what controlled Tabiq. It was all about money. She was scared as hell. Who would be the next one to step up? *It's only a matter of time before someone sees us as easy picking. Then we're the victims of circumstance all over again.*

She didn't look at it as *if* it would happen. Ziva thought in terms of *when*. She wasn't going anywhere. Tabiq was her home. It needed people like her to fight against every injustice they saw. *I might not make a big wave, but a small ripple can still rock a boat.* Ziva held her laughter. *Or even knock a badass like Rajani out cold.*

She was still shocked she'd raised her hand to someone. She'd always known there was a big boss pulling all the strings. Never in her wildest dreams would she have pictured it being a woman. *How could a woman allow this to happen to other women? Her sister?* That was what caused her to react in such a manner. It was a combination of utter shock and disgust, and years of tightly controlled emotions. *I'd trust a rattlesnake before I'd trust her.*

Rajani was only one person. There were many more

like her no one knew about. Learning to trust wasn't easy before. It was harder now.

"I don't understand. You should be happy, yet you're not," Myla said to Ziva while they took one last walk through the cabin.

"I'm happy. But at the same time, I worry about Tabiq's future. About your future."

Myla smiled. "Mr. Henderson said I could go with him to Boston. He'll pay for my schooling there. I want to be a teacher. Maybe after I graduate I can come back and teach."

Ziva smiled. "Myla, that would be wonderful. If you set your mind to it, you can do anything. You've already proven that to me."

"Thanks. I told Mr. Henderson he should ask you to come too. He said you told him no."

That wasn't exactly how it went, but the answer would've been no anyway. Boston wasn't for her, even if Alex would have asked. But it hadn't been a long lengthy discussion. She'd cut it off before he had a chance. He was an author, which meant he was a dreamer. She wasn't. Ziva lived in reality. It wasn't pretty or easy, but it was how she chose to live. If it was as easy as writing a happily ever after she would, but that wasn't the case for Tabiq. It required people who would keep others accountable. She was one of those people. *Not something I can do from Boston. I'm not sure I can pull it off living here.*

"I belong here, Myla."

"Then maybe I should stay with you so you're not

alone."

Ziva almost cried at the generous, kind offer. It wasn't one she'd let Myla do. Alex was her chance to escape and have a normal life. She wanted that for Myla, for all the girls. Tabiqians also spoke English, they'd do well if given the chance. *And Alex is that chance.* "I'm not alone."

"Of course, you are. The man you love will be in Boston. I'll be in Boston. And the other girls are going home to their families. How much more alone can you be?"

Well, that's pretty depressing when you say it like that. "Myla, I have my work. I will be fine. Trust me. And if I get time, I'll come and visit you in Boston." Although Ziva knew her so-called job at the police station didn't exist any longer, that wasn't the one she'd been referring to. Her job didn't pay in money but in satisfaction, knowing she was making Tabiq a better place. *But somehow, I'll need to find a job that pays so I can eat.*

"You promise?" Myla asked, not yet convinced.

Ziva forced a smile and gave her a quick hug. "Believe me, Myla. If I'm in Boston, I'm visiting you." It was a twist on words, but it covered her enough that it wasn't a lie.

"Then I'm leaving with Mr. Henderson tomorrow morning. I don't know what I should pack. Can you come and help me?"

Tomorrow?
So soon?

Her heart sank. She'd only had one time with him on that small island. It still hurt that he took her there, had sex with her, and then quickly accepted her answer that they didn't have a future. *Why hadn't he tried to fight for me?* It was probably better that way. The quicker, the better, they could both start to heal. It was weird with everything she'd been through emotionally *and* physically all these years, it was a broken heart that hurt the most.

"Yes, I'll help you. I have a few books about Tabiq years ago that I think you might enjoy."

"Why would I want to read about this place?"

"So that you will know Tabiq wasn't always like this. And when you dream of a better Tabiq, you can see it is possible. We once were a lovely place to live and raise a family." *A time before I was born. The times changed when my parents were young. But they remembered. They told me the stories of large families and women who were cherished by the men in their lives. Like my papa cherished my mama.*

"And you really think Tabiq can be that again?" Myla looked around the rundown cabin.

"Yes, I do."

"But how? You never saw it. I never did either. It could just be stories and not true."

Ziva reached out and grabbed Myla's hand. Giving it a pat, she said, "Just have faith, Myla. Believe it is possible. And don't settle for anything less." She wanted Myla to go on her next journey in life filled with hope and all the positive energy she could give her. By the look on Myla's face, it was working.

"Then I say we better get back and help me pack." Myla practically danced her way out of the cabin and down the path to the truck.

Ziva followed at a much slower and somber pace. She loved seeing Myla like this—full of excitement and truly happy. It was a beautiful sight, the way all young girls should be. Ziva knew Myla was one of the lucky ones. She'd been given an opportunity of a lifetime, and Myla was brave enough to take it. It showed her resilience and bravery.

Ziva refused to be anything but happy for Myla. Although they hadn't known each other long, they had bonded on many levels. *You're going to do great in Boston, Myla. I wish you all the happiness in the world. You deserve it.*

Because they were in the middle of nowhere, Ziva was used to leaving the keys in the truck. When she got to the vehicle, Myla was already inside with the radio on, singing her heart out to some pop star. She pretended to hold a microphone while belting out the words. Ziva rolled her eyes, climbed into the truck, and off they went. *Who can be blue when you're with Miss Sunshine here?*

Ziva reached over and turned the volume up, then joined Myla in one comical attempt as singers. They were laughing so hard, tears rolled down their cheeks, and their sides hurt.

Just hope and believe. I know this can be the start of a

new Tabiq. Everything will be okay. I'll be okay. I have to be.

THE DAY WENT by too damn quickly. Nothing he needed to accomplish happened. It might have been his hangover from all the beers the night before with Dean. He wasn't cutting himself any slack. The clock was ticking, and he had to move.

He was leaving in the morning, and there was no way he could leave so much unresolved. Not just with Tabiq but with Ziva. It was like she was avoiding him. The connection hadn't been in his head. He still visualized that day they were both rescued. The joy on her face to see him. The way she ran into his arms as if she couldn't bear to wait another second. He knew she'd felt it too. She was being stubborn, refusing to leave. *Why would anyone want to stay? It's an unstable society. Calm today but it could be right back where it was tomorrow.*

He hated her staying behind. When he saw Myla, he'd planted a seed. Since Ziva wouldn't listen to him, maybe she'd hear Myla. Pacing the hotel room, he figured that hadn't worked either.

Fuck it. I'll make her see me. Alex grabbed his phone and opened his room door forcefully. He wasn't expecting to see anyone on the other side, but an older woman stood before him, looking scared. *Of me or someone else?*

"Are you okay? Do you need help?"

She blinked and nodded. "I'm looking for Mr. Henderson." She choked on his last name.

Hate saying it myself. "I'm one of them. What can I do for you?"

Since Rajani had been removed from power, many people had approached him. Mostly for money, some to spit on him for who they believed he was. He had no idea what this woman would want.

She looked around in the hallway and then turned back to him. She couldn't seem to face him but asked, "May I come in?"

Alex looked her over. She didn't look like she was carrying a weapon or was a threat. Then again, Ziva hadn't either. The last thing he needed was an angry sister or cousin out to avenge what happened to her relative. Although he could certainly understand why they would.

"Listen. I don't know why you're here, but I can tell you I didn't do anything to anyone. I'm leaving in the morning and not planning on coming back. Does that satisfy your concerns?"

The woman finally looked up at him. Her eyes were filling with tears. "Tomorrow? Then please, I must speak to you today. If all I ever have is a moment of your time, it will have to be enough."

Alex didn't do well with tears. He actually didn't know any man who did. Opening the door wider, he said gruffly, "Five minutes." He knew he shouldn't be terse with her. He had no clue what horror this woman had survived, but he wanted desperately to get to Ziva, and manners and compassion eluded him.

The woman entered, and Alex closed the door. He waited for her to say something. Instead, all she did was stare at him. It creeped him out.

"Four minutes and counting." He knew he was cold, but he didn't care what she had to say. His jet was fueled and leaving first thing in the morning. *I should give her Bennett's room number and let him deal with her.*

"Please, forgive me."

Well, that's a start. For what? Who the fuck knows? Alex ran his hand through his hair in confusion. "Listen. You're forgiven. If you'll excuse me, I need to leave."

"Please, I beg you. Let me see you for just a little longer."

See me? There was something not right with this. "Who are you?"

The woman looked down again. He saw her hands tremble as she spoke. "Nikolet Maadi."

My mother.

Shit.

My mother. Zoey's aunt.

Alex legs shook and the loud pounding in his ears threw him. He hadn't expected her to show up at his door. Bennett hadn't been able to find her. "How—?"

"Did I find you?"

Alex nodded. "I have my men searching for you. That's why I'm here: to find you. No one knew what happened to you."

"A friend of yours came and saw me very late last night."

"Does this friend have a name?" He didn't have any friends here, so this was a flag. *I trust very few people.*

"She said her name was Ziva."

Alex had no idea how Ziva would've been able to find her when Bennett couldn't. *Hell, I didn't even know what her name was until last night. This doesn't make any sense.*

"Did she say how she found you?"

"No. She only told me she got my name from someone called Doug. Maybe coming here wasn't a good idea. I should go." Nikolet started toward the door.

"No!" He startled her. In a softer voice, he said, "Please come and sit. I'm sorry for being so rude to you. I just . . . I didn't think I'd get to meet you. I'd like to . . . talk to you."

Nikolet nodded and went to the couch. "You said you were looking for me. Why?"

"Because you're my mother." It was an indisputable fact.

"Yes, I am. But you're a Henderson. I am a . . . well, nobody important."

Alex couldn't sit and have this conversation. His mother was far from a nobody. Yet, he knew why she thought that. This place, the negative comments, would take its toll on anyone. "You're not a nobody. Unless you believe me to be a nobody as well."

She looked shocked. "Of course not. You are rich and powerful and—"

"Just a man. Nothing more. Money doesn't make a

person. It only determines what you can and can't afford. If anything, money has ruined more good men than I can count. You of all people should know that. My father was . . . not a good man."

"No, he wasn't," Nikolet said, her voice barely a whisper. Her hands were folded in her lap tightly.

Alex went and sat beside her, reaching out and covering her hands with his. "I'm sorry for what he did to you."

"It is not your fault."

"And it is not yours either."

She looked up at him. "Thank you for letting me see you. I have often wondered what happened to you. Your father came back several times after. I'm sure you know that."

"Yes, I do." He wasn't sure how often, but he had three younger siblings.

"I had slipped in and waited for him on one of his trips here. I had begged him to tell me about you. I knew I'd never get to see you or hold you after I gave birth to you. He'd made it very clear if I ever tried to find you, or contact you in any way, we'd both be killed." Her voice cracked as she spoke. "He held all the power. I was willing to risk myself to know you were happy."

"What did he say?"

Nikolet sobbed. "That you were and always would be a Henderson. And I'd always be nothing more than a . . . a . . . whore."

He'd grown up hearing that word. Knowing that's

what his father had called his mother felt like a knife to his heart. "I know who he was and what he called you. He was a disgusting and vile man. But, I want you to know that *I* know exactly who you are." It was the first time he'd ever had the chance to say the words. His stomach quivered, as he uttered those precious words. "You're my mother."

Nikolet burst into tears, and he pulled her into his arms. He held her while she cried. He fought back his own tears. So much time had gone by. He wished she could have held him as a boy, yet here he was the one holding her as a man. *At least, we've found each other now.*

They spent most of the night talking about her life. Her life had been very difficult. Because of their culture, she's had no husband and no other children. Although she never said it, it seemed as though she'd spent her life alone. How had Ziva known where to find her? Nothing about Ziva should surprise him. She was very resourceful. *But why not tell me? What if my mother hadn't come to me? Would you have let me leave without seeing her?* Alex hoped not, but he might not ever have the chance to ask.

Alex recalled Zoey's mother was also his aunt. *The entire situation is confusing as fuck.*

He wanted to ask about Zoey's mother, but hopefully there would be time for that. Right now was his moment with his mother. *I came here for this, and I need this time for me.*

Although he guessed she wasn't completely alone in Tabiq, it didn't change that he didn't want to leave her behind. Alex knew he wasn't staying here, but they had a lot of catching up to do. Even though they discussed a lot, he didn't feel he could leave her here in good conscience, now that he'd found her. He had pictured her living conditions many times since he'd arrived. Surprisingly, she had a small cottage outside the city where she lived alone. That word alone was what stuck in his mind. Alex wanted her to never feel alone again. For nearly forty years, this woman had been ostracized for something taken from her, and she'd had to struggle for everything she had. *While I've lived with riches and opportunities. It isn't right.*

"I would like you to come to Boston with me. Stay with me so we can get to know each other." *So I can give you what you should've had all this time. A life of luxury.*

"Oh, my son. My place is here in Tabiq. Not in America."

Alex couldn't believe it. This was the second woman he'd asked to go to Boston with him, and they'd rather stay in this hellhole. It made absolutely no sense to him. *What does this place hold except bad memories?*

"What is it with you women? Please explain to me why you'd rather be here than with me in Boston." He knew his tone was sharp, but he was frustrated.

She sighed, and for the first time he saw the family resemblance. Not to him, but his sister, Zoey, had that same look when she was frustrated with him for lack of understanding. *A look she gives me often.* He wished he'd captured it on his phone to show her. *Then I can look at it anytime I want to remember.* If they weren't discussing such a heavy topic, Alex would've taken the time to show his mother the photos of all his siblings.

"It is hard to explain or perhaps hard for you to understand. I want to be with you, but there is so much to be done here. Ziva and I had a long talk yesterday. She told me about Rajani and everything that had happened. She will not be able to stop it from happening again by herself. She will need people to help. The more people she has standing by her, the more likely things will change."

"You're staying because of Ziva?"

"Yes and no. I'm staying because this is my home. I want to help others find their way back to our old ways. The way we were before *your* father came here. What she is trying to do is admirable. If you haven't noticed, she's a very brave woman, Mr. Henderson, but still just one woman taking on a mountain of problems that need to be addressed."

"Alex. My name is, Alex."

She smiled at her son and said softly, "Alex. You should talk to Ziva."

His mother was everything his father wasn't. Warm, patient, understanding, and most of all, loving. *I want to be more like you and less like him.* "I have."

"But have you listened to her? I mean genuinely listened to what's in her heart?"

He thought he had. Now thinking back, it was more trying to convince her to see things his way, opposed to listening to her point of view. "Maybe not as well as I could've."

Nikolet shook her head. "You said you're leaving first thing in the morning?" Alex nodded. She got up. "Then I must leave now, and you must go to her before it's too late."

"Mother, what are you talking about?"

"I am talking about making things right. I know you are not your father. I can tell by the look in your eyes when I say her name she is very important to you. If you leave without listening to her, you're not doing either one of you any justice."

Nikolet walked to the door. Before she opened it, she turned to him, pulled something out of her pocket, and handed it to him.

He looked down and saw a small lace pouch tied with a very worn ribbon. "What is this?"

"All I have of you."

He opened it and found a small lock of hair.

"After I gave birth, the doctor said I could only hold you once. I stole scissors from the table, and when he wasn't looking I took a little piece of your hair. I've always carried it with me. Now that I have seen you with my own eyes, I no longer wonder. You are here. You are my son. And you are okay." She went up on her toes and gave him a kiss on his forehead. "Go to her, my son. Don't let words of your father stand between you and happiness. If you do, the joy you could find with Ziva will be lost."

Nikolet left him standing alone in his room, holding the lace pouch. He walked over to the couch and dropped onto it. *I met my mother. My real mother.* Alex couldn't stop looking at the pouch.

And she never forgot me.
She never gave up hope for me.

He wanted to see Ziva, but right now he was overwhelmed with so much raw emotion he couldn't go. If he did, he knew he'd not listen. Instead, he'd grab hold of her and beg her to go with him. His mother was right. He needed to hear her out. He knew how courageous she was, and it would be wrong to deny what her heart desired. Although, he wanted her heart to desire him. *But after that, I might resort to asking her one last time to come with me to Boston. It's where I want to be, and where I need her to be. With me.*

He grabbed his phone and texted Bennett. *Ziva's location now?*

Alex wasn't sure if Bennett was still monitoring her or not. The last instruction he'd given was to ensure her safety at all times.

His phone beeped with an address.
Everything okay? Bennett asked.
Will be.
Need backup? Bennett texted.
Nope, just a set of balls.
Got this one. See you at the jet in the morning.
Roger.

Alex got off the couch, slipped the lace pouch in his

pocket, and left to find Ziva. She wasn't as close by as he'd hoped. He was cutting it close, driving to her and still making it back in time to board the jet. *Good thing it's my jet. We only leave when I'm on board.* He really didn't care if it took off. He knew she had put up a wall around herself so she wouldn't get hurt any more than she already had been in her life. He hoped he would have had more self-control and not had sex with her had he thought she didn't want to be with him. To leave with him. But he couldn't be sure. *I couldn't resist her. I needed to taste and touch her. I want that again.* Somehow, he needed to make her understand he wasn't going to hurt her. *Not now, not ever.*

He wasn't sure what he was going to say, but he wasn't leaving until this was settled. *She's coming with me one way or another.*

Chapter Fifteen

S HE HADN'T PLANNED on driving all this way tonight but once she was in the truck, she drove until she was exhausted. She found the least questionable-looking hotel, grabbed a room, showered, and went to bed. Ziva anticipated falling asleep since her eyes had been burning, and she could barely keep them open while driving.

Somehow that all changed as soon as her head hit the pillow. She was wide awake and overthinking everything that had happened during the past couple days. She tossed and turned, then lay looking at the ceiling. She reached for her cell phone; two hours had already gone by, and the only thing she'd managed to do was spend money she really couldn't afford to waste on a room for nothing. *It felt frivolous.*

She didn't earn much money but everything she had went to provisions for the girls. Tomorrow they'd leave with Alex and she wouldn't have that responsibility any longer. *Not for them at least. I know the need here is great. So much greater than I can carry. All I can do is my best.*

No matter if she gave her last breath to secure their

safety, she still would feel as though she hadn't done enough. *How could she not feel guilty for being one of the lucky ones who avoided such mistreatment?*

Lying in bed and thinking of what she hadn't done wasn't going to help her relax. The list was endless. Thinking she'd relax if she walked around the room, she got out of bed and grabbed the sheet, wrapping it around her. She hadn't planned this little excursion, and she didn't have a change of clothes. Although she was alone in the room, she felt self-conscious. The cuts had started to heal, yet the bruises had darkened and looked worse. *There is nothing attractive or sexy about me right now. I look like I was in a brawl and lost.*

How she looked wasn't important. It wasn't like there was anyone, meaning Alex, who'd see her. She was completely and utterly alone. She let out a heavy sigh. Thinking about Alex was the reason she'd left town in the first place. She had never hopped in her truck and driven without a destination.

Tomorrow afternoon she'd return home. There would no longer be a threat of bumping into Alex or any members of his entourage. Although she had to admit, there were times it came in handy, like when Bennett and Doug told her about Nikolet Maadi. It seemed odd that two highly skilled Marines were able to find Alex and her when they were held captive, but they couldn't seem to locate one woman who wasn't hiding. *I think I was set up. Not sure why, but Doug seems very good at arranging things the way he sees fit. I think I fell right into that trap.*

Alex's brothers were nice, but they seemed to be under the false impression that more was going on between her and Alex than business. *Well, if we remove the one night on the private island and amazing sex . . . and his beautiful eyes and his sexy body. And the curl of his lips when I say something cute but he tries to hold in his laugh. Oh yeah, his corny sense of humor and his absolutely sweet and gentle heart, then yeah, we're left with only business.*

Ziva could feel her cheeks turning pink from thinking of him. *Face it, Ziva. You're not getting any sleep. Not as long as he is still in Tabiq.* It was as though she could feel him close by. *Just a few more hours, and he'll be on his way to America.*

In the short time he was here, Alex had accomplished so much for Tabiq. It meant so much that she found his mother and let her know where she could find her long-lost son.

It wasn't as hard as she'd thought it would've been. With Rajani and the manager powerless, people began speaking more freely. *Not to foreigners, but then again, those guys were pretty scary. Handy to have around, but scary nonetheless.*

When she told Nikolet why she was there, the woman collapsed to her knees, crying. Ziva bent down and held her. It had been such a touching time to bring such joyful news. She thought she'd deliver the news and leave immediately. Instead, Nikolet invited her in and begged her to stay.

It wasn't as though either of them had any stories to tell of Alex as a child. From what she knew of his past, the stories wouldn't be warm and fuzzy either. Doug hadn't told her much, but he did say being raised by James Henderson was something no child should have to go through.

The women spent hours talking about something they shared, their love for Tabiq. Ziva was surprised to learn Nikolet had been a school teacher most of her life. She no longer worked but had taught reading and writing. It was wonderful to know Alex had caught the writing bug from his mother, even if he didn't know it.

I hope you did what you said and went to find him. He needs you more than he knows. Nikolet had been nervous about meeting him, about him being disappointed in her. Ziva happily and truthfully had been able to ease her mind. *Your son is not James Henderson.*

Shaking her head of all her wandering thoughts, she gave up on sleeping. Ziva went to the chair where she'd placed her clothes earlier and dressed again. A walk in the cool night air might help. Her room was on the second floor, overlooking the parking lot. She opened the curtains and looked out the window. Gasping, she shut it quickly and stepped back. *It can't be. There is no way.*

Ziva walked around the room and turned off each light, making it appear she was asleep. She ever so slightly moved the curtain and looked again. There it was, a black SUV parked, facing the hotel. It hadn't been there when she'd arrived because she would've noticed that. Looking closer, she saw two men in the front seat. *They're definitely not guests.*

The weight that had been lifted returned. She was still being monitored. Alex may have taken out several of the trafficking leaders, but that didn't prevent her from being in danger. Ziva needed to get out of there before they found her.

If they know I'm here, they know what I'm driving. She needed a plan and didn't have time to think too long on it. Going out the front door and hopping in her truck would only mean they'd be following her to the next location. *If they don't grab me before I get there.*

Ziva remembered seeing an old beat-up Volkswagen on the other side of the building when she pulled in. It looked really rough, and she wasn't sure it would start. If it did, the owner might be interested in making a trade. Her truck, although far from new, was definitely in better shape.

She grabbed her purse and keys and went to the lobby. The person working the desk was fast asleep. *At least someone sleeps around here.*

Giving him a gentle tap, he sprang awake. "Sorry, do you need something?"

Ziva whispered, "Do you know who owns that Volkswagen?"

"You mean that beat-up thing out there?"

"That's the one."

"It was my grandfather's. He died about six months ago. It's been sitting here ever since. Why?"

"Does it run?"

"It did."

"What do you think about making a trade? I have a truck that I . . . I want something smaller. If you can get the car running and bring it to me in the back, I'll give you my truck."

"You must be crazy. Who would want that thing? I didn't even want it when my dad gave it to me."

I can see why. But it will serve my purpose. Get me the hell out of here unnoticed. "One man's junk is another man's treasure."

The kid walked away, and she heard him say, "This is why women need men. They do such stupid shit."

She could've burst out laughing. *This woman is holding things together pretty darn good, thank you. If you ask me, you're the one who should be leery about this deal. There are a few guys who aren't going to be very happy when they find you're driving my truck.*

Ziva went out back, and within a few minutes the beat-up car pulled up. She quickly scooted into the driver's seat and handed him her keys to the truck. "Good luck. Oh, if anyone asks, let them know I went for a drive up north to visit my parents."

"Sure, lady. Whatever."

That little lie would only buy her time with someone who didn't know her. People like Alex would know her parents were deceased. *But he's not the one waiting outside for me. How did they find me? Why won't they leave me alone?*

She came around the front, and she could still see the black SUV. The men hadn't moved. As she pulled out of the parking lot, she held her breath, waiting for them to come after her. She traveled a few blocks before she exhaled. *That was too close.*

It was a fact that couldn't be ignored. She wasn't as safe as she'd thought. She needed to head back to the cabin and revise her next plan of action. *At least, I only have myself to worry about right now.*

As Ziva drove, thoughts of Myla popped up. Myla had begged her to go with her to the jet tomorrow to see her off and to say one last goodbye. It broke her heart to deny her request, and Myla seemed equally hurt as well. She didn't understand how difficult this was for Ziva. No one did. *Not even Alex.*

She could lie to everyone, but she wanted to see Alex again. Her heart was ripping into pieces, knowing he was leaving Tabiq and never returning. *I hate being apart from him now, never mind for the rest of my life. But I know it's for the best.*

Myla would forgive her someday. Ziva had done all she could do for her. She encouraged Myla to follow her dream and take a chance on a new and better life. Myla had come from a good loving home that also wanted more for their daughter. Most people didn't have as much support. Not only was Alex taking Myla with him, but he was making sure her family was provided for here in Tabiq. That must've been a heavy weight lifted from her shoulders.

It said a lot about Myla's character, and Ziva knew Myla would return and fulfill her promise. She was a strong woman for such a young age. *She doesn't need me as much as I need her.*

Ziva couldn't help but wonder what her child would be like if she had one. Would her daughter be anything like Myla? Warm, loving and strong-willed? *I'd like to think so.*

When Ziva was young she pictured what most girls did, getting married and having a family. Yet when that age came, she had to turn away from her heart's true desire. *Help the girls of Tabiq.*

It hadn't been a popular path. She recalled when she told her parents what she was planning on doing. She understood the resistance she met was out of love. No parent wanted to think their child would potentially face danger every day for people who'd never know her name.

Her mother had begged her to let others take on the fight. She'd said they hadn't hidden her away for so long, only to end up losing her. Yet, almost ten years later, and Ziva was still fighting for her cause. Alone. *I just wish my parents were still alive to see the day Tabiq was given a second chance.*

Because of her choices, she was now twenty-nine and single. She couldn't remember looking back and wishing she had more. Somehow, because of one man, more was what she wanted now.

Can I think of any more depressing topics? She knew she had to snap out of this. It'd been her decision not to go to Boston. Regretting made no sense at all. *Wishing he'd come and ask me one more time also made no sense. My answer wouldn't . . . couldn't change. Tabiq needs me. It's all I know.*

Ziva had no idea how she'd made it back to town. She was supposed to have turned off the road miles back. After all, she'd intentionally left to get away. It was ironic, but she believed the car—though not her own—had traveled as if on autopilot. She knew it was her self-conscience telling her what her heart wanted. She didn't want to hear it. Her head was in charge, and returning here was a poor choice.

The sun was beginning to rise, a beautiful multi-colored orange. That meant another hot day on the way. *Yet another reason to get out of here.* She found out quickly that the hunk of junk didn't have a radio or air conditioning. It was tolerable during the night, but once the sun rose full blast in the late morning, she'd melt sitting there.

Although she didn't want to be in front of Alex's hotel, she couldn't bring herself to drive away either. She needed one last look at him, even if it was from afar. *Better that way.*

Everything was quiet; it felt eerie. Ziva looked around and noticed their vehicles were gone.

I . . . I missed him. He's gone.

Her heart began to race.

He's gone.

He's really gone.

Ziva felt tightness in her chest. It was panic.

Tears rolled down her cheeks. *Since when did I become an emotional wreck? I don't cry, yet I seem to cry all the time now.* Of course, her tears weren't for nothing. The man she loved was going to board his jet, and she'd never be able to tell him how she felt. Throwing the car in drive, she floored it. Surprisingly the little car still had some life in it. The tires squealed as she sped away. *I can't be too late. I just can't be.*

She made it to the outside edge of town before steam spewed from the hood. Ziva pulled off the road and slammed her fist into the steering wheel. *Damn.* There was no way she could drive to the airport like this. The engine would blow long before she made it. The only thing she could do was walk back to town and see if someone—anyone—would give her a ride.

The one problem? People weren't going to drive her anywhere close to the Hendersons. *Well, one might, if she's not with them already.*

"WHAT THE FUCK? You're being paid to watch Miss Gryzb. How did she get past you without her truck?"

"Sorry, Mr. Henderson. We were told to make sure no one hurt her. We didn't realize she'd sneak out in the middle of the night."

"Do I look like I want an apology or your lame excuses? The only words I want to hear from you are that you found her. Do I make myself clear?" Alex barked his orders to the guard who was still by the SUV. He was livid, and not just at them, but at himself. He hadn't warned her he'd left a security detail to make sure no lingering goons came after her. If he had, she could've reached out to them when trouble came her way.

It's been less than twenty-four hours since we parted ways, and something has already happened to her.

Alex, still holding his cell phone, tried her number again. Just like the last time, it went directly to voicemail. *Please let it be a dead battery.* He slid the phone into his back pocket as the second guard came out of the hotel saying, "I've checked everywhere. Her room is vacant and the old man at the desk said he didn't see her leave."

Alex knew there was no way she left with someone. She'd have gone kicking and screaming. *At least, the woman I know would've.* "Someone knows something." He looked around and saw a small house next to the hotel. *I wonder.*

He started walking in that direction when the first guard shouted, "Want me to call for backup?"

If I don't find her, you're going to need the protection. From me! Alex shook his head and continued walking. He knocked on the house door, and a young man in his late teens answered rudely, "Unless you're blind, the hotel's office is over there. Can't miss it. *Big* red letters. Unless you can't read either."

Punching out some bratty kid wasn't his thing. "I'm looking for a woman who was staying here."

"I have a *don't ask and don't tell* policy. What your wife does is none of our business."

Alex's jaw twitched with anger. "I have my own policy. You watch your mouth, or I'll make it so you drink from a straw for a year." The kid straightened and backed up a bit. "Want to try this again?"

The kid nodded.

"Her name is Ziva Gryzb. She was driving that truck when she arrived. Did you see who she left with?"

"Oh, that crazy wom—" He held up his hands in a mock surrender, as he knew it was a mistake. "I mean, that lady said to tell anyone who came looking for her that she traveled up north to see her parents."

Her parents are dead. Why try to throw us off? "Was she on foot, because her truck is here?"

"Hell, no. She traded me for my Volkswagen. It's not in great shape, so I'm surprised you didn't pass her broken down on the road."

Alex remembered seeing one in bad shape when he was driving here. It'd been traveling south toward town, not north as this kid said. "Was it gray?" *Clever woman. She planned to send whoever she thought was watching her the wrong way.*

"The parts that aren't covered in rust are. Hey, don't be angry with me. The cra . . . the lady insisted. She looked like she was afraid someone was watching her. Like her life was in danger. Is she hiding from you?"

Alex didn't reply. Instead, he pulled out his phone and called Bennett. "She's in an old gray Volkswagen. I passed her about an hour ago heading toward town. Find her."

"Already have the choppers in the air searching."

He went up to the two guards and said, "You two better pray we find her. If *anything* happened to her because of your incompetence—"

Still on the phone Bennett shouted, "Get the facts first, Alex. We'll find her."

Alex shot the two a warning look and walked away with his fist clenched. If he hadn't, all his frustration would've been taken out on them.

"Get a chopper here to pick me up. I don't want to waste any time driving back," Alex ordered Bennett.

"ETA ten minutes."

He slipped the phone back into his pocket and went back to his vehicle. He couldn't be around anyone right now. Alex needed time to process everything that'd transpired since his feet touched down in Tabiq. It felt like the country was cursed. *Or was that just him?*

He knew this was his fault. Coming here would stir things up and it sure as hell had. When he found out what she was doing, he should've insisted she stay with him while he was in Tabiq . . . and then *hopefully* come with him to Boston for good. But when she put up resistance, he caved too quickly. Not because he didn't want her with him, but he didn't feel as though he was good enough. *Why would she want a Henderson?*

It was what had been on his mind the entire way here. Ziva had proven time and time again what a resilient and resourceful woman she was. Although there was so much to see and do in Boston, he knew she'd feel like she was in a cage, that her purpose in life had been snuffed out. Alex might be nine years older than she was, but Ziva was doing something with her life that was actually making a difference. *She's trying to make this world a better place and all I do is write fiction, attempting to hide from anything real. You can't get more real than she is. She's . . . one hell of a woman.*

Just because she was strong didn't mean she didn't need him. *God knows I need her.* She'd shown him more about who he was in a short time than he'd been willing to admit. All these years, he'd run from being a Henderson instead of working to make the name something to be proud of.

You've become very important to me, Ziva. Where the hell are you? I need you to know what you mean to me.

When the chopper landed, Alex hopped in, and the two guards joined him, leaving their vehicles behind. It took all his self-control not to tell them to get the fuck out. None of them had expected Ziva to take off like she had. But he needed everyone he could find to look for her.

The bird was in the air not even five minutes when the pilot handed him a headset.

"We located the car on the side of the road just outside of town. You weren't joking when you said it was beat-up. I can't believe it made it that far."

"Any sign of her?" Alex asked Bennett.

"There are footsteps heading to town. We're on it. Alex, don't worry, we'll find her."

God, I hope so. "We're on our way." It was still early, so the heat hadn't fully set in yet. If they didn't find her, and she was walking for more than an hour, she'd quickly overheat and dehydrate.

"We have people on the ground, checking in the town."

"Thanks. Keep me posted."

He wasn't sure where he should start looking. Alex hadn't explored the town much at all, unlike Bennett and Doug who'd scoped out everything. They were his best hope of locating her.

The sun was up, and as they flew over houses he saw people already up and on the move. There was a mother walking with small children in tow. He couldn't help but wonder what it would've been like to grow up here, instead of in Boston with his father. They didn't have the financial benefits of living in the lap of luxury, but they had something he didn't. A true family unit.

This is what Ziva is fighting for. It was something he'd always wanted. He needed to find her. If nothing else, he'd make sure she was safe and tell her he wanted to help her.

Exactly what that help would be he wasn't sure. The government was a mess, and the country was understandably very rocky. It was going to take some serious work to get it stabilized again, never mind become a safe place to live. He respected everything she was trying to do, but it was impossible to do any lasting good by herself. *It's going to take money and manpower. She has neither.* Fortunately, he had both.

He tapped the pilot for the headset again. Once in place, he called out to Bennett. "It's a long shot, but I think I know where she went."

"We'll take it 'cause we're striking out."

Alex gave him the address of his mother's house, thankful he'd had the forethought to get it from her. Since Nikolet had told him Ziva had been there once, maybe she'd go again if she needed help. *It's worth a try.*

"Alex, you realize she's on foot. That is a lot of distance for someone her size to travel."

"Bennett, you underestimate her." *A mistake I've made myself. She is capable of more than any of us give her credit for.*

"Roger. On our way."

So am I. Alex gave the pilot directions where to head next. The pilot nodded and the chopper banked hard to the right with the new coordinates. Odds were Bennett would arrive before him. He wanted to be first, to have her rush to him and throw her arms around his neck, kissing him like she had those days ago. He hoped she would be as happy to see him as he was her. *Then again, nothing I've played out in my head has turned out how I envisioned it. Why would this be any different?*

Rather than dwelling on what might or might not be, he went with his gut. And that told him if Ziva couldn't be with him, she'd go and be with Nikolet. Bennett was right, it was a long shot, but so was coming halfway around the world to find someone like her. If she wasn't with Nikolet, he'd keep looking until he found her. There was so much left unsaid, and he wasn't leaving Tabiq until it was all out on the table.

I need to see you. Hold you one more time. Tell you that I . . . His heart was racing. *That I love you.*

Chapter Sixteen

"OH DEAR, COME inside. You look exhausted." Nikolet opened the door and gave Ziva a tender, motherly hug.

Ziva wrapped her arms around Nikolet's waist and didn't let go. She couldn't believe she made it. When she decided to leave the main road and cut through the woods, it sounded like a smart thing to do. It provided shade so she wouldn't overheat, as well as kept anyone from grabbing her off the trail.

She never would've left the woods and come to Nikolet's home if she thought she'd been followed. *Whoever thought they had me will have some explaining to do to their boss. I've been hiding in the shadows for most of my life.* Ziva wasn't sure she knew how to function any other way.

Ziva felt safe for the first time since she'd spotted the black SUV at the hotel. Every vehicle she'd passed on the road had spooked her. Then, in the woods, she'd looked over her shoulder every time she heard the rustle of branches. It felt good to be here, safe, in the home of

Alex's mother. *Even though Alex didn't grow up here, or with Nikolet, I feel as though I'm close to him here.*

As the two women finally released their hold of each other, Nikolet took her by the hand and led her into the kitchen. It was where they'd spent hours chatting the last time. "Let me get you something cold to drink while you sit and tell me why you're here." Nikolet didn't turn around as she added, "I would've thought you would be with my son."

"I was thinking the same thing about you when I knocked on the door." Ziva had wanted to see Nikolet again, but after all the years they'd spent apart, she thought Nikolet would go with him to Boston. Filled with concern, she asked, "You did see him, right?"

Nikolet turned with a smile that shined all the way to her eyes. "Yes, my dear. I saw him last night. We had a . . . lovely time talking."

Then her eyes glistened, and Ziva hoped something hadn't gone wrong. When she'd told Nikolet about Alex, she wanted it to be a joyous occasion. She never thought it might cause her pain as well. *That's because I'm not a mother and was only thinking of the instant connection, not the goodbye.*

She couldn't begin to understand how Nikolet was feeling. It was breaking Ziva's heart not to be with Alex. She could only imagine how a mother would feel. *No matter how many times mothers had to face the cruelty of having a daughter taken away from them, the pain never got any easier. I can see it in the faces of the women. The dead look in their eyes, a black hole that will never be filled.*

"I'm sorry. I didn't mean to upset you." Nikolet forced a smile, but Ziva could see the pain written all over her face.

"You haven't. I'm so grateful you came to me and told me my son was here."

"I thought maybe he'd have asked you to go with him to Boston." *If you were my mother, I never would've left you here.*

"He did."

"Then why are you not on the jet with him?" Ziva was shocked.

"I almost did. If I hadn't met you first, I most likely would've been."

"Me? What did I do?" Ziva didn't remember saying anything bad about Boston or Alex.

Nikolet reached out and patted her hand. "You opened my eyes to what Tabiq can be again. You gave me hope. Something I had lost."

Ziva's eyes welled up. "I know it can be a place to be proud of again. It's going to take—"

"More than just you. With me here, we are at least two."

"You mean you stayed to help me?"

Nikolet shook her head. "I stayed to help Tabiq. The same as you."

Ziva understood. "Thank you, but do you realize what you're giving up?"

"Not as much as you are."

She raised a brow. "I don't understand. The son you've wanted for almost forty years is back in your life."

"I had no control of what was taken from me. I can't get that lost time back. All I can do is live in the moment. Alex will always be in my life, in my heart, whether we are in the same country or not. Rest assured, my dear, we'll keep in touch."

"I'm sorry for what you lost, but I'm glad you finally have each other now."

"It's none of my business, but you, my dear Ziva, why are you letting go of the man you love? He isn't being ripped from your arms. *You* are sending him away. I fear it's going to be the greatest regret you carry when you reach my age."

It was something she battled over and over. She wanted to be with him. *And I do love him.* "It's not that simple. We're from two different worlds. I don't fit in his." *And he doesn't want to be in mine.*

"I may not have married, but that doesn't mean I don't know what love is. It is a life of its own. His hopes and dreams become yours, and yours become his. You don't give up one for the other, but together you blend your natural gifts and help each other be the best you can be. I truly believe if you're not a better person with a spouse, then you're with the wrong spouse."

The way Nikolet presented her view on love was very beautiful. It touched Ziva's heart, and she wanted to believe she and Alex could've had that. *But it's too late. He's gone.*

"I guess we'll never know." Although she tried, her voice didn't hide her own heartbreak.

There was a knock on the door and Nikolet got up to answer it. She said, "Sometimes you have to open a door and let love in so you can find out."

When she opened the door, Nikolet stood back, and Ziva could see Alex standing there. He entered the room and headed right toward her. Out of the corner of her eye, she saw Nikolet leave the house and close the door behind her.

You're smooth, Nikolet. I know where your son gets his gift of words.

"I can't believe you took off like that."

It wasn't the welcome Ziva had anticipated. Seeing his handsome face again warmed her heart.

He wasn't the only one surprised either. She knew his jet was supposed to leave at sunrise. Yet he was standing in front of her, only inches away, and it was sweeter than honey. "I thought you were gone," Ziva said breathlessly.

"You think I could leave without knowing you're safe?"

Her heart sank. *He's still leaving. This visit is just another goodbye.* In a much softer voice, she said, "I guess not. So you see I'm safe. Now you can go."

She hadn't meant for her voice to sound so pitiful. The last thing she wanted was for Alex to know how ripped apart she was. After all she'd experienced in her life, she was a strong woman. *So why don't I feel strong now? Why do I feel like pulling a blanket over my head and crying until the pain is gone?*

"Is that what you want, Ziva? For me to walk right back out that door?" Alex looked at her so intensely she couldn't bring herself to look away.

"I don't know." It was the truth. Part of her wanted him to be here with her, but she didn't want him living the life she lived. *This place is not a dream. It's a nightmare. One I can't wake from. Why would I want the man I love to share such a fate?*

Alex reached out and touched her cheek. "Were you crying?"

A tear or two may have sprung free when she was talking to Nikolet. *When I realized what I wanted and knew I couldn't have it.* "Your mother and I were talking about . . . Tabiq."

"Yeah. This place would make most people cry." He didn't remove his hand as he continued, "Tell me what about Tabiq brought tears to your eyes, Ziva."

That you won't be here with me. "All the work ahead of me . . . us."

"Us?" Alex asked, cocking a brow.

"Yes. Your mother and me. She's going to help me."

"Just the two of you?"

"Two is better than one."

He pulled his hand from her and paced the room. "I don't like this. There is no way I'm leaving you two when this country is so unstable. Who the hell knows what crazed maniac will step into power next?" He turned back to her and asked, "What do you think is going to happen to both of you then?"

"The risk is no different than it always has been."

"And you think that makes me happy?" Alex barked.

"There are more important things than being happy." *As long as I'm separated from you, I don't think I'll ever be happy again.*

"Are there more important things than your safety? If you ask me, the answer is no."

She knew he was trying to show he cared. It was obvious, and she was being a jerk by pushing him. "I don't have a death wish. Yet, what I've been doing and what I need to do next is important. You know that. Think of your mother. What she's been through. I don't want any other woman to face such hardships. This is not about me, or what I want, it's about what . . . I have to do." Ziva reached up, and this time she touched his cheek. "Please, Alex, try to understand. And don't hate me for staying."

Alex pulled her into his arms and squeezed her so tight she thought her ribs would break. "Sweet, I couldn't hate you if I tried. Staying here scares the hell out of me because all I want is to keep you safe and make you happy. Back in Boston, I know I can do both. Here, I'm not sure."

"Alex, no one can guarantee safety. The world is changing. Even here we see the news. Evil has taken root in the most innocent neighborhoods. All one can do is live their life, and treat others the way they want to be treated. Everything else is out of our control."

"I won't ever sleep with you here and me there."

"I can't leave."

"Then it's settled."

"I guess it is," Ziva answered softly.

Alex put a finger under her chin and tipped her head up to meet his gaze. "We stay in Tabiq."

She blinked. Stunned and not sure she heard correctly.

We?

Ziva knew she was tired and her emotions were playing tricks on her mind. There was no way Alex Henderson told her he was staying.

"You heard correctly, Ziva. If you won't come with me, I'll stay with you."

"Why?" The question was so simple, but such an important one.

He chuckled. "For one of the most intelligent women I know, do you really need me to tell you?"

Yes.

I need to hear the words.

"Alex, I don't want to have misread anything."

Alex smiled at her. "Then, my sweet, let me clarify for you. I am staying with you because I can't picture my life anywhere but with you. I know we haven't known each other very long, but in that short time, for the first time in my life, I want to be a better person, and I want to be that person because of you and what you've made me feel. I love you, Ziva Gryzb. And if this is where you want to be, then here is where I'll be. Your fight is now mine. Besides, if you think two are better than one, can you imagine what three can do?"

Ziva couldn't think past the words I love you. "Say it again."

"What part?"

"That you love me," she said, smiling and beaming from her toes to the top of her head.

Lifting her off the floor so they were face to face he said, "I love you more than I ever thought possible. What do you say about facing our tomorrows together?"

"I'd like that."

Pulling her even closer he lowered his voice. "Is that a yes?"

She hadn't recovered from him telling her he wanted to join her on her mission in life. Everything happened so fast she needed to slow it down a bit. There was no question in her mind that she loved him. Spending the rest of her life with him would complete her. This wasn't something he should rush into. She wasn't sure she'd heard him correctly in the first place. "Wait, what was the question?" She hadn't heard one that required a yes or no.

"Not very romantic, I know."

"Alex, it's not about romance. I don't want you to feel . . . pressured . . . in any way. You can stay here with me, and we can do this together. You don't have to mar—"

Alex kissed her briefly, muffling her words. Then he

let her slip from his arms. Instantly she wanted to throw herself back in his embrace. It was the one place she felt safe. *Loved.* She hoped she didn't push him away. The walls she kept around herself so she couldn't feel pain were the same walls she'd built so she couldn't feel love. Since Alex entered her life, the mortar had cracked and each stone had been removed. He was in, and without him there, the void would be impregnable.

When she stood on her own two feet, he dropped down to one knee.

"Ziva Gryzb, will you marry me?"

Her heart was pounding so fast, she barely caught her breath. This man's name was synonymous with much torment for her country. A name that to this day instilled fear and caused mothers to hide their children. How could she consider taking that name as her own? *But this is not just any name. It's Alex's.*

With tears rolling down her cheeks she choked out the word, "Yes."

Alex peered at her. He was still on a bent knee, so he gave her a slight tug, bringing her closer as she now sat on his knee. Now they were eye to eye. "You hesitated. Are you sure?"

"It's just that this is so different from Boston. I'm not sure you'll be happy here." *We're not the rich and famous. Well, not famous for anything good.*

"There is plenty here that I want to do myself."

"Like?"

"I found my mother. Or I should say *you* found her.

My siblings don't know theirs, and I want to locate all of them. It's going to be difficult for all parties involved. I know what I felt, and I can't imagine what my mother is feeling. I could use your help with finding them and the transition to meeting their children."

Ziva grinned. He genuinely wanted her to be part of his life. Not just here, but to become part of the entire Henderson family. She'd already met two of his brothers. If the rest were as kind, she knew she'd love them. *And hopefully, they'll love me in return.*

"Alex, I'd love to help you. Thank you."

"For what?"

"For trusting me."

"My sweet, I should thank you for trusting me. I know what my name means here."

It was sad but true. They were hated. *Unless you were greedy and only wanted their money.* "Alex, that can change. I actually believe it has started. It will take time, but the people will see the man I see. And they'll feel the same way."

"And how is that?"

She smiled. "They'll love you."

He kissed her gently. "I don't care who loves me, as long as you do."

"Well, Mr. Henderson, I do love you, and in case you have any doubt, yes, I'll marry you."

Alex kissed her again. This time so tenderly it made her yearn for more. She pulled away and reminded him gently where they were. He laughed and said, "I can't help but lose myself when I'm near you."

Ziva got off his knee and said, "Maybe we should find someplace more . . . private."

"Ah, like my island."

"Your island?" Ziva asked.

"Yes, the one I took you to. I thought we could build a home there. You know, travel back and forth for times when we need a little . . . quiet."

"And how are you going to work there?"

"I'm an author, Ziva. I can work anywhere."

"Even here?"

"I might find some inspiration here."

"I'd be flattered if you told me you wrote romance instead of intrigue," Ziva teased.

"Hmm. Let's get out of here," Alex said, dragging her to the door.

Following him out of the house, they saw Nikolet sitting on a bench. Alex turned to Ziva and said, "Give me a minute."

She nodded. *I'll give you my lifetime.* She watched as he went to his mother. They spoke briefly but from the look on Nikolet's face, Alex told her what transpired. She stood, placed a kiss on her son's forehead, gave him a hug, then sat back on the bench. When Alex turned toward her again his eyes were sparkling.

"Mother said welcome to the family," Alex said as he took hold of her hand again.

She'd gone a long time without family. "I'm so happy you found each other."

"No Ziva. You found both of us. Without you, none of this would've been possible. Not stopping Rajani or the manager. Finding my mother probably would've taken more time, and who knows how receptive she'd have been without you? I call you my sweet for a reason. Because life has been noting but sweet since I laid eyes on you."

She wanted to remind him about their little hostage situation, but looking back, it was something they'd shared together. Therefore, she'd agree, it was sweet.

They held hands as they headed down a path that led to a small field not far away. There was a chopper in the clearing, waiting for them. She must've been deep in conversation with Nikolet to miss hearing its approach.

Alex didn't slow his pace as they continued to make their way to the chopper. He seemed focused. On what she didn't know. "Is something wrong?" Ziva asked, perplexed with the sudden change.

"Nope. I was just thinking about changing genres and needing research."

"What genre?"

Alex spun around and swooped her high into his arms. "I was thinking erotica."

Her eyes widened. "You want to write that?"

He shook his head. "Nope. Just do the research."

"What exactly do you have in mind?" Ziva asked him seductively.

Alex came close to her ear and whispered, "To love you from head to toe and then start all over again. Unless you have any objections?"

"A lovely way to spend a night."

"I was thinking five nights."

"Five?"

"For starters." Ziva arched a brow then Alex continued. "If I thought I could keep you away from here longer, I'd have said a month, but I know how anxious you are to get back and begin your work."

"I'm that obvious?"

Alex nodded. Giving her a nip on her earlobe, he asked, "Are you with me?"

His for five nights? Yeah, it's a good start. She liked this playful side of Alex. It was refreshing after all they had been through. Ziva laughed. "Till death do us part."

She leaned close to his ear and whispered a dirty little desire she had. Alex stiffened and said, "Oh, yeah. A lot of research will be needed."

As he carried her to the chopper, Ziva knew everything wasn't perfect. They would face many difficulties, and the mammoth effort to rebuild Tabiq could possibly be heartbreaking. But what was different now was neither would face them alone. For so many years, that had been all she'd known, and knowing she had two people by her side, her heart soared. She'd probably lost her job after being gone so many days, but then again, with Alex by her side, maybe they could have an actual police department that *upheld* the law instead of breaking it. The possibilities for the future were endless. All because one man, Alexander Henderson, would be by her side.

Today, right now, they were happy, and she was going to learn a new lesson. *I'm going to live in the moment and hold on tight.*

Tomorrow would come soon enough, but today all she wanted was to be Alex and Ziva. *And one day, Mr. and Mrs. Henderson.*

The End

Don't miss book 6, After Six!

Be the first to hear about my releases
www.jeannettewinters.com/newsletter

Other Books By Jeannette Winters

The Billionaire's Secret

Billionaire Jon Vinchi is a man with one passion: work. His friends decide to shake him up by entering him as a prize at a charity event.

Accountant Lizette Burke is dressed to the nines and covering for her boss at a charity event. She's hoping to land a donor for the struggling non-profit agency that employs her.

She never expected to win a date with a billionaire.

He never thought one night could turn his life upside down.

One lie stands between them and their happily ever after. Too bad it's a big one!

Betting on You Series:

Book 1: The Billionaire's Secret (FREE!)

Book 2: The Billionaire's Masquerade

Book 3: The Billionaire's Longshot

Book 4: The Billionaire's Jackpot

Book 5: All Bets Off

Book 6: A Rose For The Billionaire

One White Lie

Brice Henderson traded everything for power and success. His company was closing a deal that would cement his spot at the top. The last thing he needed was a distraction from the past.

Lena Razzi had spent years trying to forget Brice Henderson. When offered the opportunity of a lifetime, would she take the risk even if the price would be another broken heart?

Do you love reading from this world? Continue with Always Mine from my sister, Ruth Cardello, Her series will mirror my time line. It isn't necessary to read hers to enjoy mine, but it sure will enhance the fun!

Barrington Billionaires Series:

Book 1: One White Lie
Book 2: Table for Two
Book 3: You and Me Make Three
Book 4: Virgin for the Fourth Time
Book 5: His for Five Nights
Book 6: After Six (Coming 2018)

Southern Spice

Derrick Nash knows the pain of loss. But is he seeking justice or revenge? He doesn't care as long as someone pays the price.

It is Casey Collin's duty at FEMA to help those in need when a natural disaster strikes. After a tornado hits Honeywell, she finds there are more problems than just storm damage. Will she follow company procedures or her heart?

Can Derrick move forward without the answers he's been searching for? Can Casey teach him how to trust again? Or will she need to face the fact that not every story has a happy ending?

Southern Desires Series:

Book 1: Southern Spice

Book 2: Southern Exposure

Book 3: Southern Delight

Book 4: Southern Regions

Book 5: Southern Charm

Book 6: Southern Sass (Coming 10/13/17)

Books by Ruth Cardello

ruthcardello.com

Books by Danielle Stewart

authordaniellestewart.com

Do you like sweet romance? You might enjoy Lena Lane www.lenalanenovels.com

Made in the USA
Middletown, DE
25 January 2018